He was…bigger than she remembered. More muscular. Taller.

He wasn't *GQ*-handsome. He was more of a tough, I'll-do-what-I-please kind of man. Something about it attracted her. Or would have if it hadn't been Zach Rundle.

"Thanks for coming so—"

"You didn't give me much choice did you?"

She straightened and inched forward. "Believe me, if I weren't so concerned about your nephew I never would have called."

He sized her up, trying to decipher her motives. She was a far cry from the teenage girl he remembered. He'd been turned on as hell by her then, but this version of Lindsey had his thoughts going in all kinds of directions he hadn't allowed them to go in a long time. He'd grown up, gotten serious. He was no longer a sucker for a pretty face.

Especially not in this godforsaken place.

Dear Reader,

When our first child was born, I was a typical nervous parent. Actually, I far surpassed that and was extremely uptight. Mostly because I believe parents can have a profound effect on their children and who or what they grow up to be.

I took this idea a step further in writing *The Boy Next Door*. I wondered what kind of effect a parent's *death* could have on three sisters, especially if the girls were teenagers when it occurred. Let's face it, being a teenage girl isn't easy anyway, but throw such a traumatic event at them...and what becomes of them later?

How does it affect their future relationships? With their immediate family? With men?

In *The Boy Next Door,* you'll get to know Lindsey Salinger and how her mother's death influenced who she is at twenty-eight. It caused problems that she's been able to ignore or at least avoid for years...until she falls in love with Zach Rundle.

Falling in love forces Lindsey to face up to hard truths. She learns that to find joy in her future, she must put the past to rest. Of course, a lot of things are a tiny bit easier when there's a ruggedly handsome man in the mix, especially when he happens to be right next door.

I hope you enjoy Lindsey and Zach's story. I love to hear from readers, so feel free to e-mail me at amyknupp@amyknupp.com. Or stop by one of my online homes: www.amyknupp.com or www.writemindedblog.com.

Amy Knupp

THE BOY
NEXT DOOR
Amy Knupp

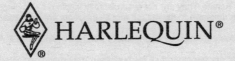

HARLEQUIN®

TORONTO • NEW YORK • LONDON
AMSTERDAM • PARIS • SYDNEY • HAMBURG
STOCKHOLM • ATHENS • TOKYO • MILAN • MADRID
PRAGUE • WARSAW • BUDAPEST • AUCKLAND

ISBN-13: 978-0-373-78147-8
ISBN-10:   0-373-78147-4

THE BOY NEXT DOOR

Copyright © 2007 by Amy Knupp.

This edition published by arrangement with Harlequin Books S.A.

www.eHarlequin.com

Printed in U.S.A.

ABOUT THE AUTHOR

Amy Knupp lives in Kansas with her husband, two sons and three cats. She graduated from the University of Kansas with degrees in French and journalism and feels lucky to use very little of either in her writing career. She's a member of Romance Writers of America and shares a blog with four other authors (www.writemindedblog.com). In her spare time she enjoys reading, buying books in excess, traveling, watching college basketball and playing addictive computer games. For more about Amy's books and writing life, visit her Web site at www.amyknupp.com.

Books by Amy Knupp

HARLEQUIN SUPERROMANCE
1342–UNEXPECTED COMPLICATION

For Carol Knupp, who loved stories, written and spoken. We miss you and all the stories you told.

Acknowledgment

A big thank-you to Kristin Bell, Lisa Mooney and Jill Weigel. You ladies were so patient and helpful in answering my endless questions about social services.

Sharon, Jan, Anjana and Jill, your awesome critiques and brainstorming are invaluable. Without you, I'd be curled up in the corner muttering nonsense phrases.

Karen D....the Lazy Goat would be nameless if not for you. I bow down to your bar-naming expertise.

Mom and Dad, thanks for telling everyone you know (and then some) about my books. If you're proud of me, read the reader letter and know I mean what I say about parents.

Victoria, thank you for one mark-free page! In all seriousness, your edits are invaluable and make the story so much stronger. Thanks for the countless hours you put into it.

Justin, thank you for putting up with me, cooking, helping me plot, cooking, believing in me and cooking. You're the absolute best husband (and a darn good cook!).

CHAPTER ONE

LINDSEY SALINGER FREQUENTLY found herself doing the ill-advised, all in the name of helping someone in need.

Like now. The ill-advised was jogging—fast—when she hadn't exercised for a while. Okay, a long while.

The someone in need was her dad. She had to check on him, see for herself he was following doctor's orders and doing what he was supposed to: staying horizontal. His live-in housekeeper, Mrs. Hale, had been with him all day, but she'd had to leave for a meeting.

This would be a lot simpler if Lindsey's 1996 Civic hadn't quit on the way home from work. Since she'd already been running late and her roommate, Brooke, wasn't home, she'd decided jogging was the quickest way to get there. If she didn't die first.

Three houses down from her dad's, she allowed herself to slow to a brisk walk. She sucked in the chilled air in an attempt to dull the pain in her lungs. As she blew out, a sound from the evergreen bushes bordering the sidewalk stopped her.

Was that a child's whimper?

She strained to hear, wondering if her ears were playing tricks on her. But no, she heard a shaky intake of breath from the same direction. Faint, but unquestionable.

Lindsey looked at her dad's house, searching for a sign that he needed her immediately, but of course, there was none. No movement, no noise, only a dim light on inside.

She crouched to scan under the low-hanging branches and thought she spotted something on the far side. Creeping forward, she saw two small feet in grungy once-white socks.

"Who's there?"

No reply.

Lindsey ducked her head and pushed

her way through the branches. Her hands sank in the cold dirt, and pine needles stuck to her clothes.

Once she reached the trunk, there was a little more clearance, and she sat up as much as she could. She shoved her ball cap back to find herself face-to-face with a boy who couldn't be much more than five or six years old.

"Hi," Lindsey said, smiling to ease his fright. "It's okay. I'm one of the good guys."

He sized her up for several seconds, and she wondered if he'd try to run off. There was no quick escape route, so she doubted she'd lose him.

The boy's dark hair was disheveled, and he wore only a long-sleeved shirt, jeans and socks. Not nearly enough for February in Kansas—it couldn't be more than forty degrees out here. He clung to a branch near his head with one hand and grasped a small toy truck in his other.

"My name's Lindsey. What's yours?"

He sucked in his lower lip and let out a wail.

"Come here, sweetie." She held him while he sobbed into her shoulder.

Why was this little guy outside by himself?

He grabbed her upper arm with his free hand, squeezing tightly. Lindsey rubbed the back of his head with a gentle, circular motion.

She'd have to take him with her to make sure her dad wasn't curled up with a bag of chocolate chip cookies or something else off-limits.

"Shh. It'll be okay."

The boy's sobs gradually slowed, and he let go of her arm. He rubbed his eyes with one hand but still held the yellow cement mixer as if his life depended on it.

"What's your name, sweetie?"

He didn't respond; instead, he turned and scooted several inches away.

"Are you lost?" She reached across and rumpled his hair. "Tell you what. Let's get you inside and warmed up. You like hot chocolate?"

He shrugged.

"I bet you do. With mountains of whipped cream on top."

She saw a flicker of interest in his eyes.

"Then you can tell me your name and where you belong."

Please, let him open up. She didn't want to call the police. They'd just rattle him further.

"Come with me."

They crawled out from under the branches. Lindsey brushed dirt and twigs off her own pants, then the boy's. She held out her hand. He hesitated, then took it, and Lindsey frowned at how cold his fingers were.

The spicy aroma of burning cedar wood nearby hovered in the breeze and Lindsey shivered. She'd dressed lightly for running—yoga pants and a long-sleeved T-shirt—not for a kid rescue.

They'd passed two yards drenched in shadow by towering, decades-old oak trees before the boy spoke. "Where are we going?" His voice was hoarse, like he'd been crying for ages.

"To my dad's house."

He seemed to consider her answer for several seconds. "Do you live there, too?"

Lindsey shook her head. "I have my own

house, so I don't live with my dad any-more."

"Me, neither." His voice was consider-ably quieter, melancholic.

Where was his mother?

When they reached her dad's, she slipped her left, rarely worn tennis shoe off and took out her key, then unlocked the front door. She stomped her shoe back on as they walked through the main floor. A faint light shone under the closed door of the den, which they'd converted to a tem-porary bedroom so her dad could avoid stairs. Good. At least he was where he was supposed to be.

"Hey, Dad, it's me!" Lindsey said as she went by. "Be in in a sec!"

She led the boy into the large kitchen of the house she'd grown up in and flipped on the fluorescent light.

He darted a curious glance around the room, shifting his weight from one leg to the other.

"Can you tell me your name now, sweetie?"

He studied the floor, running one foot

along the lines in the linoleum pattern. "Owen."

Her heart missed a beat.

Coincidence? She could only hope. She'd heard rumors around town for the past couple of weeks about a boy named Owen.

Thank goodness her dad's door was shut. She lowered her voice. "Is Josh Rundle your daddy?"

He nodded solemnly.

Oh, God.

Lindsey's chest tightened. She didn't realize she'd clenched her teeth until the pressure became painful and registered in her brain.

No.

She pushed the hateful feelings aside and compelled her body to relax. Pretend Owen belonged to someone else. He had nothing to do with his father's past.

She had no idea what her dad would do if he found out she'd brought a Rundle into his house, but she knew it wouldn't be good. He couldn't afford to get upset, especially not with his health so fragile.

Forcing a smile, she patted Owen's head and went to the fridge to make him a snack.

She sliced an apple and some cheese and warmed a mug of instant cocoa in the microwave, hoping the food would keep him occupied while she went to say hi to her dad.

Josh's child. That would explain a lot. Why he was left to wander outside, why he was underdressed. Why he was scared, hungry and tired. Josh Rundle didn't have a responsible bone in his body.

Lindsey set everything on the table, spooned whipped cream into the mug and pulled the chair out for Owen. "I'll be right back," she told him. "You stay here and fill your tummy."

She went to the den-turned-bedroom, which was next to the kitchen. She knocked lightly on the door but didn't wait for a reply.

"Hey, Dad." She made her voice cheerful as she entered the room, every surface cluttered with books and newspapers. Her eyes automatically stopped at the Astros cap—her favorite—in the top row of his wall of baseball caps.

Her dad, in flannel pyjamas, raised the remote from his stomach and muted the television. "Hi, honey," he said as she leaned down to kiss his forehead. "Didn't hear you come in."

"How're you feeling?" She scrutinized him for a sign that he should still be in the hospital.

Wendell Salinger's salt-and-pepper hair seemed heavier on the salt than it had been just a week ago and was rumpled from being in bed for days on end. His hazel eyes moved from her to the silent television and back again. That he was watching TV instead of reading spoke of his fatigue as much as his red-rimmed eyes did. The frown etched into his face seemed more pronounced than usual.

"Oh, not bad, all things considered."

All things considered were a heart attack and a double bypass eight days ago. Lindsey had brought him home from the hospital just this morning. She'd hated leaving him right away to rush to work, even though he had Mrs. Hale, who served as her dad's live-in housekeeper, cook and friend. Mrs. Hale was kind, caring and took no crap. Lindsey trusted Claudia Hale as much as the wonderful nurses who'd mollycoddled her dad the past few days, but she still needed to be here herself.

"Sorry I'm late."

He furrowed his bushy dark eyebrows. "Late? We have a date?"

"I told Mrs. Hale I'd be here before she left for her church meeting."

"I don't need a nursemaid."

She sat on the roll-away twin-sized bed next to him. "Did she make you a good dinner?"

"Hell, no. Didn't give me enough to fill up an ant. I want a slab of meat, not a scrap."

Lindsey sighed. "She was following doctor's orders. You can't eat like you used to."

"You'll take care of me though, won't you?" He smiled confidently.

"Of course. I'll make you follow your new diet."

He started to say something, but she cut him off.

"No grumbling. You're going to do this our way. We'd like to keep you around for a while."

His face softened and he reached for her hand. "I'd be more grateful if you'd bring me a hunk of that chocolate cake I saw on the counter out there."

"Dream on. The Nelsons didn't know chocolate cake is off-limits now. I'll be sure to take it home so it won't tempt you anymore."

Lindsey felt a tug at her shirt hem and looked down to find Owen right next to her.

"Can I have more snack?"

"What's going on?" Her dad's voice was level but the pained look in his eyes told her he knew this was Josh Rundle's son. He'd probably seen Owen around—Owen's scum-sucker dad lived with his grandma, right next door.

According to talk around town, Owen's mother had recently died in a car accident, and authorities had tracked down Josh, who hadn't known he had a kid.

"I found Owen in the Abrahams' yard. Apparently lost."

Wendell swallowed hard and looked away. So much emotion crossed his face that Lindsey's chest tightened. She hated to see her dad hurting.

Lindsey picked up Owen, as if she could protect her dad by taking the boy out of the room. "I'm taking him home now."

"Careful, honey." The warning in his tone made Owen lift his head off Lindsey's shoulder.

She made a quick exit, setting a frowning Owen on the kitchen floor when they got there.

"Why do you have to be careful?"

"Dads just worry a lot, sweetie."

He nodded. "More cheese?" he asked.

"It's 'more cheese, please.' We need to get you home. I bet your dad wonders where you are."

"He's not there."

Color her not surprised. "Where is he?"

"I don't know. Grandma says he runned away."

"How long has he been gone?"

"Lots of days."

Interesting. But not out of the realm of possibility where Josh was concerned. She'd have to see what information she could get next door.

"Let's go see Grandma Rundle, then."

Lindsey grabbed one of her dad's heavy

jackets off the coat tree by the back door and hurried Owen out the front. She paused on the top step.

"How old are you, Owen?"

"Five." He held out a hand, fingers spread.

"You're a pretty big boy, but why don't I carry you so your feet stay warm." She lifted him, then brushed his dark hair off his forehead. "You have shoes at home?"

He nodded. "Red Power Rangers ones."

"Sounds cool." She tickled his tummy. "Next time you want to play outside, you be sure to put your shoes on, okay? And ask your grandma first."

He nodded, and she noticed dark circles under his eyes. She'd bet he was about to collapse. Who knew how long he'd been outside? She gritted her teeth.

Lindsey carried Owen across the two adjoining front lawns, which had turned brown and crunchy for the winter. When she'd been a girl, she'd always thought the Rundle house was the best on the block with its Victorian trim, giant front porch and light yellow paint. Now it showed its age and a lack of TLC.

After ringing the bell, they waited on the front porch for someone to answer. Seconds ticked by. If the house hadn't been lit like a laboratory, Lindsey might have concluded the Rundles were gone, maybe out looking for Owen. But she heard a thud inside, like someone dropped something. Then a string of curses loud enough for Lindsey to decipher clearly. Still, no one answered or even came into sight through the window in the front door.

She rang the bell again and heard another thud. At last she saw Mrs. Rundle's withered face peek around a corner inside. She squinted, disappeared, then reappeared, tottering toward the door.

Lindsey braced herself for the woman's sharp tongue. The heavy front door opened and the old woman peered out at her, her gray eyes wary. Lindsey waited for the flash of recognition, which would promptly be followed by trademark crabbiness.

It didn't come.

Mrs. Rundle studied her for several seconds, then turned her attention to

Owen. She took in his appearance for a good five heartbeats.

"Sugar, what are you doing outside?" She addressed the boy warmly, then threw an embarrassed half grin toward Lindsey as she opened the storm door. "It's cold out there, Joshua. Come let Grandma warm you up."

"Owen, Grandma," the boy said.

Mrs. Rundle stared at him in confusion. "What?"

"I'm Owen."

"Of course you are."

Lindsey set him down inside the door and followed him in. Heck if she was leaving without trying to find out what was going on. "I found him huddled under the bushes in the Abrahams' yard. No shoes or coat."

"Why were you outside, sugar?" The woman bent and kissed Owen on the forehead, affording Lindsey a view of pink scalp through white wispy hair. "I thought you went upstairs to watch a video after dinner."

Had Owen been roaming around by himself for an hour or two?

"It got over," Owen explained.

"He loves his Power Heroes video." Mrs. Rundle addressed Lindsey with a polite smile.

Lindsey faltered. She felt as if she'd entered an alternate universe. She hadn't known this woman was capable of smiling. Not at her, anyway.

"Rangers," Owen corrected. "Power Rangers."

Owen's great-grandmother grabbed his hand, and the two of them started to walk down the hallway.

"Mrs. Rundle?" The woman seemed to have completely forgotten she was there.

When Mrs. Rundle turned to look at her, the politeness disappeared, replaced by a scowl. "What do you want?" Any confusion that may have been there before had also disappeared.

"Owen told me his dad wasn't here. When will he be back?"

Mrs. Rundle looked troubled, her weariness evident. "His dad?"

"Isn't he Josh's son?" She hated even saying the words.

The older woman's face looked strained for a moment. "Yes."

Lindsey's instincts screamed that something was off here. "Where is he?"

"He's not here. I take care of the boy now."

"I see." She studied the woman's somber face. "Mrs. Rundle, are you okay?"

Thin eyelashes fluttered over her dull eyes. "I'm fine," she rasped into the awkward silence. "Leave us alone."

Lindsey watched Owen and decided he had no qualms about staying with his great-grandmother. He still clung to the woman's hand and looked up at Lindsey expectantly, as if waiting for her approval.

She reminded herself her approval wasn't required here. The questions she was programmed to ask as a caseworker weren't her concern this time. Owen wasn't one of the kids she was assigned to help.

But her case or not, his well-being *was* her business—she'd make it hers. Was this moody woman capable of seeing to Owen's needs? Based on what she'd witnessed in the past five minutes, she wasn't anywhere close to convinced.

AN HOUR LATER, LINDSEY was still mulling over Owen and his great-grandma as she drove her dad's extralarge, old-man car back to her house. Something was definitely wrong.

She parked in the street, then ran up the creaky wooden stairs to the front porch and let herself in. Brooke was still awake, judging by the smells of cooking coming from the kitchen.

Lindsey went in to say hello and grab a snack—something not as healthy as what Brooke was sure to be cooking.

"How's your dad?" Brooke asked, standing in front of the stove.

Lindsey set her dad's chocolate cake on the counter, then stood on tiptoe to rummage through the cabinet above the fridge. "He wasn't too bad until he saw Owen Rundle." As she grasped a bag of jelly beans, she briefly related the tale of finding Owen and her dad's reaction to the boy.

"So Josh split, huh?" Brooke watched her and stirred some kind of egg concoction in a large skillet.

Lindsey poured herself a handful of candy, then shrugged. "Apparently."

"You don't seem as happy as I'd expect."

She moved closer and looked over Brooke's shoulder. "Why are you making enough eggs for an army at ten o'clock?"

"I missed dinner. So?"

"So?" Lindsey sorted through the jelly beans in her hand, grouping them by color, and stuck three green ones in her mouth.

"Josh? You think he's gone for good?"

"Most likely, now that there's a reason for him to stick around." She couldn't keep the disgust out of her voice as she ate the red jelly beans next. "But Owen's probably better off with him gone. If only his great-grandma can hold it together."

Brooke flipped the stove off and dumped a bowl of grated cheese into the eggs. "What's he like?"

"Owen? Nothing like you'd guess Josh's son would be. Cute. Quiet. Likable."

"Poor kid."

Discussing Josh made Lindsey's stomach turn, to say the least. "I need a shower." She popped two yellows into her mouth, dumped all the black jelly beans in the trash and headed for her bedroom.

As much as she didn't want to think about her run-in with the Rundles, she couldn't get it out of her mind. She tried to put a finger on what was going on. Mrs. Rundle had offered no further information on Owen's dad, but knowing his reputation for letting people down, it was likely he'd taken off and deserted his kid. How anyone could do that to a child, she'd never been able to understand. She saw it all the time on the job and it made her want to pull her hair out—people who didn't value their children above everything else. How did they justify that in their minds?

She didn't get it. But then she also didn't understand how Josh could live with himself in the first place.

The most disturbing thing, though, aside from finding Owen all by himself, was that it hadn't seemed as if Mrs. Rundle knew who Lindsey was at first. But that was impossible. She'd watched Lindsey grow up, ever since the Salingers had moved in when Lindsey was six years old.

The phone rang, startling her out of her thoughts. She tossed her cap on her cluttered dresser and grabbed the extension from the nightstand by her bed. "Hello?"

"You make it home?"

The gruffness in her dad's voice made her smile. "Of course."

"Don't give me that. Crazy people out there, even in Lone Oak. You've got to be careful."

"I'm careful. It was a two-minute drive." She sat on the double bed to take off her shoes and socks. "Don't worry about me."

"Lindsey, listen to me. Don't get involved with those people."

"Dad—"

"I know how you are, honey. You have to jump in to rescue those in need."

"I'm not rescuing anybody. I took Owen back where he belongs."

"You're getting involved. I can feel it."

"You want me to ignore my instincts?"

"I just worry about you. I wish you'd stay away from them."

"I can't do that, Dad. I don't trust that family to take care of Owen."

She heard the concern in his sigh even over the line. "That's what I was afraid of."

"I'm just going to make sure he's okay. I have to."

"Watch yourself, would you?"

"Mrs. Rundle isn't going to scare me away from making sure Owen's well cared for. But I'll be careful. Did Mrs. Hale give you your ten o'clock round of pills yet?"

"What do you think?" he grumbled.

She laughed. "I think she'll do fine keeping you in line."

"Keep yourself in line. 'Night, honey."

"'Night, Dad."

Lindsey turned the phone off and tossed it onto her unmade bed before crossing the hallway to the bathroom. After turning the shower on, she undid her ponytail and absently brushed tangles out of her long brown hair, waiting for the water to heat.

Was an eighty-something woman really able to take care of an energetic boy? Especially a woman who'd seemed disoriented?

Occupational hazard, she told herself, shaking her head. She stepped into the stream of hot water, running options through her mind.

It wasn't a case for social services—yet. Not something for her to take on professionally. Sadly, it took a lot more to warrant that kind of attention, thanks to cutbacks in budget and staff.

Right now, a family member needed to get involved. The only one she knew besides Josh was his brother, Zach.

Her stomach took a nosedive at the thought.

Lindsey hadn't spoken to Zach for… almost thirteen years. Not that she was counting. Whenever she heard he was visiting his grandma, which wasn't often, she made a point of staying away from her dad's house. She'd run into him exactly twice—somewhat inevitable in a town of less than five-thousand people—but they hadn't spoken. She'd had nothing to say to him.

Speaking to Zach was about as appealing as ripping her toenails off one by one.

But, damn. She didn't have any choice.

Not if she really had Owen's best inter-
ests at heart. He was the only one who
mattered in this.

She had to forget how she'd completely
embarrassed herself with Zach that night
years ago. And somehow totally block out
the fact that his brother, Josh, had driven
the car that had killed Lindsey's mom.

CHAPTER TWO

ZACH SLID BACK IN THE perpetually dusty chair across from his boss. "What if the planning commission doesn't approve the zoning changes? What do we do then?"

Charles Moxley, his mentor since he'd arrived in Wichita nearly thirteen years ago, stretched his arms behind his head. The aged man's faded sweatshirt popped up and would've revealed a round white belly if not for the thin T-shirt tucked into his jeans—Zach had seen it happen so many times he barely registered it now.

"They *have* to approve it," Chuck said, determined as usual. "Danged government types would be fools not to."

"Stranger things have happened."

"You just worry about getting your facts down pat for the meeting Monday night.

With all the research we've done, they've got to listen."

"I'll be ready. Don't you worry about it."

Chuck lowered his hands to the desktop with a smack. "Ain't worried at all. You've never let me down." He beat his hands on the desk as if it were a drum. "You're getting so uptight about things here, I think you worry more about the business than I do."

Zach grinned. He had a lot at stake with Moxley Construction, maybe even more than Chuck did anymore. "Don't want you running this company into the ground before you sell to me. You know how old folks get." He pushed back his chair and stood. "We'll get this approved, no problem. Won't take no for an answer."

They couldn't. Zach had been in on the original purchase of the land in question—one hundred acres on the outskirts of Wichita. They'd sat on the property for years, waiting for the right time to develop it into an upscale neighborhood of homes and businesses. The time was now. Unless someone on the commission didn't see things the same way.

"I'm off to the Harrison site first, probably be there until early afternoon. Then I'll be at Prairie Acres. Gotta wait for an inspection. If they don't get there today, we'll have problems."

Chuck stood and hefted up his jeans, then saluted. "I'll sit in the office and be useless, as always." He chuckled, but Zach knew staying away from the action, as Chuck called it, bothered his boss. After his dreary health report last spring, his wife had banned him from job sites and physical labor, the parts of the job Chuck loved most.

If Zach could do something to change that, he would. He owed the man everything he had. The luckiest day of his life had been when Moxley had taken a chance on a rebellious, angry eighteen-year-old with enough attitude to choke an army sergeant.

He'd given him the job as a trial. Two weeks. One screwup and Zach was out of there. Fortunately, he'd passed the test and had worked his way up the company ranks. When Moxley retired in a couple years—or sooner if his health got worse—

Zach was set to buy the company from him. Finally, he was *this* close to making something of himself. Not bad for the outcast from Lone Oak.

Zach stepped up into his truck and was about to put the key in the ignition when his phone rang.

"Rundle," he answered tersely, wondering what crisis had cropped up at the site so early.

"Zach Rundle?" The melodic feminine voice caught him off guard. Women didn't call him if he could help it.

"This is Zach."

"This is Lindsey Salinger. From Lone Oak."

The past and the town he hated came storming back to him in a barrage of memories. Images of the accident that had killed Mrs. Salinger flashed through his mind, threatening to bring back feelings Zach had locked away twelve years ago.

"Hi," he said, wondering what she could possibly want.

"I'm sorry to bother you…" He heard her inhale, felt her hesitation. "I'm worried about your…grandma…and your nephew."

His heart dropped. "What's going on?" He wasn't sure he could handle bad news about Gram. He'd convinced himself she'd be around forever.

"I'm not really sure. I found Owen outside last night, huddled under a bush crying. No one had noticed he'd been gone…for a while."

Instantly, relief flooded him. Gram wasn't in immediate danger. It took a few seconds for him to register what else she'd said, though, and who Owen was. His nephew. Zach had yet to meet the boy and had a hard time imagining any offspring of his brother.

When he'd heard of the kid's appearance at his grandma's house, he'd just shaken his head. Unfortunately, Josh and trouble went together like peanut butter and jelly, and a child popping out of nowhere was definitely trouble.

When they were growing up, he and Josh had proudly shared the "bad boy" crown by being general nuisances, but Josh had more than taken over the title in the past decade or so. After the accident, Josh's life went to hell. He was aimless, drank more than his share and now he had a kid to worry about. Zach hated to see it, but didn't know how to help him.

"Where's Josh?"

"Gone, apparently."

"Gone where?"

"No idea. Hasn't been seen for a while, from what I gather." The intensity of her dislike for his brother struck Zach in the chest. He couldn't blame her, though.

Dammit. This was exactly the stuff he wanted to avoid. Remembering. Feeling.

"I haven't heard from him in weeks," he said. They were close enough, but they didn't keep tabs on each other.

"He left Owen with your grandma."

Her tone said that should explain everything to him. Call him dense, but he didn't get the problem. His grandma had served as both mother and father to him and his brother, and she'd done the best she could. Child care was nothing new to the woman. Even if she *was* getting up there in years.

"They'll be okay."

"That's just it… I'm not convinced. I took him home last night and your grandma… she didn't seem well."

"Didn't seem well, how? What's wrong with her?" A rush of possibilities filled his head.

"She seemed disoriented. I don't think she knew me at first." Lindsey paused. "Put it this way—she was *nice* to me for the first five minutes I was there. She let me into her house. She had no idea Owen was missing."

Being nice to Lindsey *was* an oddity for Gram, but not cause for him to drop everything and run home. And there'd been plenty of times when he himself had pulled one over on Gram by slipping out the back door. "Owen's a boy. Boys sneak around and cause trouble."

"He's only five, though." He heard background noise, another person talking, Lindsey saying she'd be just a minute. "Zach, I'm the last person who wants to butt into your family's business, but you need to check on your grandma. Age can affect people differently."

Something in her voice caught his attention. Was she insinuating Gram was losing it? No goddamn way. His grandma might be old, but she was one strong woman.

He'd visited her for Christmas, and she'd been sharp as a knee to the nuts.

"What are you trying to say? You want me to come to Lone Oak?"

"I'm saying I'm worried about your nephew."

"I don't get it. Why would you care about Josh's kid?"

"He's a little boy. Someone needs to make sure he's okay, that he's getting the care he needs. His father sure isn't. He's got a lot working against him."

"If Gram is there, he's fine." It really was that simple.

"Check on your grandma, Zach. If you don't, I will."

So the grown-up Lindsey was pushy, aggressive. He wished he could say that turned him off. "Is that a threat?"

Her voice was softer, but not calmer. "I'm giving you fair warning. I intend to make sure Owen has a competent guardian. If something were to happen to him, we'd all be sorry."

We? Since when did she care about anything Rundle? Not that her lack of faith surprised him. Most of Lone Oak held his family on about the same level as mud.

Lone Oak was the last place he wanted to be, but he wouldn't let anyone, pretty face or not, mess with his grandma. He exhaled loudly, pinching the bridge of his nose. "I'll be there late tomorrow."

He shut his phone to end the conversation. If she so much as breathed a word of her off-base ideas, the whole Podunk town would be whispering about his grandma before he could pack a bag and gas up his truck. He'd bet this was nothing more than her trying to get back at Josh, but he couldn't sit by and ignore it. Even if it meant coming into contact with Lindsey Salinger again.

AGITATION HAD BEEN simmering since her phone call to Zach this morning. What was it about him that made her edgy? He didn't take her seriously, that's what it was. He doubted her competence and her sincerity. Made her feel like a child trying to cause trouble.

She stood in her dad's kitchen, heating a mug of water in the microwave. Mrs.

Hale was here tonight, but Lindsey liked giving the woman a break. The housekeeper wasn't paid well enough to be her dad's nurse on top of everything else, even if she insisted she enjoyed helping him.

Lindsey frowned as she watched the digital numbers tick down. Zach had always made her feel like a child, even though he was only two years older than her.

If he thought she could be insensitive enough to hold Josh's sins against an innocent child...well...just the idea burned her to the core. What kind of a person did Zach think she was?

In truth, she supposed he had absolutely no idea what she was or who she was. They didn't *really* know each other, not beyond the names and reputations a small town had built for them—and an evening of ill-advised liberties in an old, dusty wood shop she wished she could forget.

Still. That he would treat her with suspicion gave her the urge to break something. Possibly his neck. She knew Owen hadn't been in the family for long, but surely Zach had an ounce of caring in him and didn't want any harm to come to the child. Did he?

It came back to the same thing—she didn't know. She didn't really know him, either. Sure, she once thought she knew him, thought she'd seen some redeeming qualities in him. But that was a lifetime ago. He'd still been a boy, and she, a naive girl searching for a hero. Had she ever searched in the wrong place.

She'd made every effort to know as little about Zach as possible since he'd left town. She wouldn't care if he were the governor of Kansas. She had nothing to do with him anymore and never would.

Or at least she wouldn't once this situation with Owen was cleared up.

Lindsey stirred tea for her dad, after adding a generous dollop of honey, then carried it to his room.

He eyed the mug suspiciously. "What're you going to make me choke down now?"

"Brooke says it's good for your immune system and healing. I sweetened it up for you."

She held it out to him but he didn't budge. Setting it on the nightstand, she bent to kiss him. "Drink it by the time I get back."

"Brooke's tree-hugging home remedies are going to be the death of me, not my faulty ticker."

She chuckled. "Drink it."

"Where you headed?"

"You don't want to know."

He didn't say a thing, just got quiet and looked morose.

"Owen left his cement mixer here last night. I'm taking it back. If you hear gunshots, call 9-1-1 and pray that old bat's a bad shot." She hurried out the door, wishing he'd laugh at her attempt at lightness.

Lindsey grabbed the truck she'd found under the kitchen table and went out the front door. Hopefully Josh was still gone.

Unlike the other night, when she and Owen had cut through the grass, Lindsey walked all the way around on the sidewalk, heading for the driveway on the far side.

She rolled her eyes, remembering all the times Mrs. Rundle had hollered at her and her sisters for being on her precious crabgrass-ridden lawn. It was as if she'd watched out the window for the slightest infraction. Before the accident, the relationship had been more neutral, but since then, there'd been nothing but tension. Elsa Rundle's mission seemed to be to make sure no one looked on her grandsons badly. No matter that at least one of them might deserve it. It had probably crushed Mrs. Rundle when Josh had done time for his crime.

As Lindsey ascended the slight incline on the Rundle driveway, she heard someone in the backyard. She followed what sounded like feet thudding onto gravel every few seconds.

She found Owen jumping from the back concrete stairs into a dormant flower bed filled with small white rocks.

"Hi, kiddo." She smiled as he raced to the top step to leap again.

Jump. "Hi!" He didn't slow down to talk to her, heading back up the stairs.

"What are you up to?"

Jump. "Exercising." *Pant, pant.* He gave the task everything he had.

"Careful not to fall." She moved closer

and took the opportunity to hold out the yellow truck when he landed again. "Look what I found in my dad's kitchen."

His eyes lit up when he saw it. "I thought it was lost forever!" He rushed toward her and grabbed the toy. Without so much as stopping to breathe, he skipped to the pavement, dropped to his knees and assured himself the truck still drove right.

"Is your dad home yet?" If he was, she was outta there.

"Nope."

"Does your grandma know you're outside?"

"Yeah."

Lindsey glanced toward the closest window, expecting to see narrowed eyes glaring at her, but there was no one there.

"I'm glad she knows where you are. That way you won't get lost." Or cold, she thought, although he did have a jacket and ratty Power Rangers shoes on.

Lindsey wasn't completely comfortable walking off and leaving Owen by himself outside, but she didn't have any choice. Mrs. Rundle must be checking on him from the window periodically. Owen appeared to be fine—no signs of the lost, scared boy she'd come upon yesterday.

"I have to go now, Owen."

He halted his noisy narration of the cement truck's progress across the driveway and glanced up at her with a long face. Darn if this little guy didn't get to her, in spite of who his family was.

Those eyes begged her to stay a while longer. Five minutes of her time was nothing, and she could handle Mrs. Rundle if she had to. Kids needed interaction and playmates, and she'd bet a month's salary Owen didn't have much of either. "You want to play for a few minutes?"

The slow smile that crept across his face was worth the risk. "You like hide-and-seek?"

She nodded.

"You be 'it.'"

"Yes, sir. Stairs are base." She knelt on the bottom step and ducked her head into her arms. Closing her eyes, she counted to twenty in a loud voice.

Owen became more animated with each round, and she loved seeing him open up. They'd both hidden several times when she started to think she was pressing her luck. "You hide one more time, then I have to go. My dad's waiting for me."

"I'm gonna find the goodest place this time!"

She laughed. So far she hadn't had any trouble locating him. He had a hard time staying quiet.

After counting again, she warned him she was on her way. For once, she didn't hear a giggle or the scuff of shoes on the ground. She was sure he wasn't in the immediate area.

She glanced around the backyard and didn't see him peeking out anywhere, so she headed toward the front of the house. Wandering slowly along the driveway, making a show of looking everywhere in case he was watching, she wondered aloud where on earth a sneaky boy could hide.

She was almost to the front corner of the house, searching in the line of evergreen shrubs along the driveway, when a big, black testosterone-ridden truck whipped into the driveway, skidding to a stop just in time to avoid hitting her.

THE ONE SHE WAS BORN

CHAPTER THREE

LINDSEY'S HEART restarted as the driver got out and slammed the door. She glanced around to make sure Owen hadn't emerged from hiding and witnessed her nearly becoming a pancake. She was relieved to see no sign of him.

Her relief smacked into a brick wall as Zach Rundle strode around the front of the truck toward the side of the driveway where she'd scrambled.

She felt herself shrink and stepped back as he approached. He was…bigger than she remembered. Broader. More muscular. Taller.

She could tell herself until she was dizzy from lack of air that he wasn't more appealing than she recalled…but she'd be flat-out lying.

He wasn't *GQ*-handsome. He was more

of a dark-haired, tough, I'll-do-what-I-please kind of man, but it looked good on him. Something about it attracted her. Or it would if it wasn't Zach Rundle.

He gave off an air of boldness, as if he knew he could handle anything—and maybe had during his lifetime. She knew his childhood hadn't been particularly rosy, but he definitely didn't look any worse for the wear.

"You okay?" he asked.

"Just perfect, thanks."

"Sorry about that. I wasn't expecting anyone on the driveway."

"So I noticed. There's a child living here, you know."

He started to respond, then closed his mouth.

The moment she'd dreaded for years was finally here, and it was every bit as awkward as she'd imagined. Worse. Because he was being nice.

She wished she could forget about how he'd humiliated her years ago. How he'd sent her away. But sixteen was an age where girls were easily scarred by rejection. Here it was, years later, and his still stung.

Lindsey's mouth was suddenly parched. She moistened her lips. "Thanks for coming so quickly—"

"You didn't give me much choice, did you?" His tone carried a hint of annoyance.

She straightened and inched forward. "Believe me, if I wasn't tremendously concerned about your nephew, I would never have called you."

He sized her up, seemingly trying to decipher her motives, as if she were hiding something. The only thing she hoped to hide was how he made her feel like she'd been shot back in time.

Zach stepped forward, not taking his eyes off Lindsey. It was a stare down. She definitely had the advantage on that one, as he felt slightly off-balance just being close to her.

She was still a beauty. Still had the looks of the town sweetheart, of the girl who could do no wrong. Heart-shaped face with skin like fresh peaches and cream, brown eyes with a glimmer of spirit in them, prominent cheekbones and long brown hair that'd been tossed around by the wind. The only thing missing was that damnable dimple. As long as she didn't smile, he'd be okay. And at the present moment, she didn't seem to be much in a smiling mood.

"I'm still trying to figure out why you *did* call me. Why would you care about anyone in my family?" He kept his voice steady. No need to show how unraveled he felt.

She whipped her hair back behind her shoulder, clueing him in to the fact that she was upset. Welcome to the club.

"Your grandma could have a serious problem. Dementia. Alzheimer's. Something entirely different. Family members are often the last to admit there's anything wrong."

What kind of psychobabble was she rattling on about? What did she know about families and dementia and…and then it hit him. She was a social worker of some kind. He remembered hearing it vaguely—one of the thousands of downfalls of coming from a town too small to piss in—you heard stuff you didn't want to know about people you tried not to think about even once you'd moved on.

"We don't need social services, so you can quit hovering like a vulture, waiting to swoop in."

Her eyes flashed with emotion. "My job has nothing to do with my concern for that boy. He's a sweet child who deserves more than he might possibly be getting."

A dark-haired kid popped out of the bush at the end of the driveway and came barreling toward them. "You didn't find me! I'm gonna make it to base!" he sing-songed as he zipped past.

Lindsey took off after him, letting him beat her. Once they hit the back steps, they both collapsed in laughter.

"I winned! I winned!" The kid Zach assumed was Owen bounced on the bottom step, pleased with himself. Lindsey congratulated him with a hug. Zach could tell she was used to being with kids. The total opposite of him.

"You're too good for me, Owen," she said. "That was a tricky hiding spot."

She gave Owen a high five. Zach felt like an outsider standing by the home where he'd grown up.

He watched the kid with concealed

interest, unable to fully grasp he was Josh's flesh and blood. Zach's nephew. Owen seemed full of energy and in no danger. He was scrawny, but then, Zach and Josh had both been rail-thin as kids, too.

Lindsey, on the other hand, wasn't rail-thin. Her modest curves and tiny waist were apparent through the snug fit of her sweater and jeans. She was a far cry from the teenaged girl who'd approached him in the backyard shop. He'd been turned on by her then, but this version of Lindsey threatened to send his thoughts in all kinds of directions he hadn't allowed them to go in for a long time.

Zach had grown up, gotten serious. Figured out the important things in his life. And a woman wasn't one of them. He was more interested in practical, uncomplicated things, like his career. He was no longer a sucker for a pretty face or a fantasy-inspiring body. Especially not one with such a load of emotional baggage, who lived in a godforsaken place he would never call home again.

The back door was out of sight from

where he stood, but Zach heard the old screen door squeak open.

"Owen! Come over here! Salinger girl, get your skinny butt off my property!"

Lindsey's eyes closed and even from where he stood he could see her take a deep breath. She didn't give his grandma a glance, but bent down to Owen. "See you, kiddo. I had fun playing with you." She smiled warmly at the boy, giving no obvious sign of being bothered by the scolding.

She used to burst into tears with the slightest provocation—he'd witnessed it several times from afar. Gone was the girl who wore her heart on her sleeve. In her place was…definitely a woman.

No. He couldn't think of her that way—as the opposite sex. She was simply the nagging inconvenience that had dragged him away from Wichita for a few days.

Zach walked up the driveway toward the back door, and their eyes locked. For an instant. Sparks of challenge and, dammit, attraction, shot between them. Once she'd passed him on her way to the sidewalk, he turned around to check out the skinny butt his grandma had mentioned. Then he turned away, reminding himself he didn't want to think of her that way.

"Zachary Rundle! What the peewaddin' are you doing here?"

He grinned up at the crotchety old woman, then took the steps in two bounds to deliver a hug. "Grandma."

She felt frail in his arms, not quite as strong or full of it as she'd always been. Seeing her get older and weaker was rough, but still, it was always good to be with her again. Whenever he came home, he realized how much he missed her. He couldn't stand the town, but he loved this old woman.

When they pulled apart, he could swear he saw a hint of moisture in her eyes, but by the time he did a double take, it was gone. Good. She wasn't going soft on him. That wouldn't be his grandma.

"You didn't answer my question, mister."

He squeezed her shoulders, unable to stop smiling.

"So this is Owen, huh?" He motioned

over his shoulder, then turned to the boy who stood glued to the bottom step, clearly confused.

"This is Owen. Owen, say hello to your uncle Zach."

The child looked down at his feet and didn't respond.

"Owen." Grandma's voice was sterner.

He mumbled a "hi" so soft Zach barely heard it. Maybe the kid wasn't as outgoing as he'd originally thought.

"I don't think he's used to men," his grandma said quietly.

"Hey, O." He paused, wondering what one said to a five-year-old kid. "How you doing?"

"Fine."

He glanced at his grandma, hoping she'd take charge as was her specialty. Nowadays, Zach was comfortable with that for the most part. But when he was a teenager, there'd been plenty of head-butts.

"Come inside, Owen. You need a bath," she said.

"I'm not dirty." The boy searched his arms and trunk and shrugged his shoulders. The earnest look on his face almost made Zach chuckle.

"*Now*, Owen."

Zach was quite familiar with Gram's don't-mess-with-me tone, and he waited to see if his nephew had figured out she meant business. Owen plodded up the outside stairs to the back door, shoulders sagging. Either he learned fast or he was used to taking orders from his great-grandma.

Zach followed them inside to the kitchen.

"Where's Josh?"

"Don't go jumping into questions until you answer mine. What are you doing in town?"

"Couldn't stand being away from you any longer, Granny Dearest."

She grabbed a magazine off the ancient white countertop, rolled it up and bopped him on the head. "Don't you sweet-talk me, Zachary." She grinned in spite of her tough act.

"Owen, go get your dirty clothes off. Uncle Zach will be up to run some bath water in a few minutes."

The boy flew out of the room, probably glad to get away from the uncle he'd never met before. Zach shrugged. He knew what it was like to have a bunch of new adults forced on you after your parents took off. He distinctly remembered it sucked.

Zach hefted himself up onto the counter next to the sink. If Owen didn't want to open up to him, so be it. Zach didn't consider himself much of a talker, anyway. Besides, he wouldn't be here for long. Just long enough to get Lindsey off his grandma's back.

"Where's my shit-for-brains brother?" Zach said lightly.

"Zachary. There's a child in the house. Try to restrain yourself." Her lips puckered in sternness and he felt like hugging her again.

"So where is he?"

His grandma's face fell and she shook her head as she lowered herself onto a ladder-back chair. "Wish I knew. Least he could've done is leave a note."

"Yeah, I can see Josh as the note type." He shook his head. If Josh had ever done anything responsible in his life, their grandma would look ten years younger. But her devotion to both her grandsons had never wavered.

"How long's he been gone?"

"Over a week. He's never left for this long before, not without telling me."

The grave look on her face told him she was worried. And she didn't worry easily. She'd raised her own two boys and then him and Josh as well. Raising boys, especially Rundle boys, wasn't for the faint of heart.

"That's too bad. Instant fatherhood probably did him in." For a moment, he wondered where his brother might be hiding out. Then he noticed his grandma staring at nothing, her forehead furrowed. "Is anything else wrong, Grandma?"

Her head jerked toward him sharply. "Why do you ask?"

Zach shrugged. "Just making sure. You're not a spring chick anymore, much as you like to think. A five-year-old's a lot to handle." He hopped down from the counter and pulled out the chair and sat. "You doing okay, Gram?"

He watched her throat move as she

swallowed before answering. "I'm not dead yet, Zachary. I can handle that boy just fine. Compared to you and your brother, he's a walk in the park."

Her answer soothed any fears he may have had. He doubted there was anything wrong outside of Lindsey Salinger's imagination. However, one thing still nagged at him.

"Lindsey said you were nice to her when she brought Owen back the other day."

His grandma considered his words for some time and scowled. "So? I'm old enough to decide when I want to be friendly. She brought the boy back."

That made sense. She couldn't be rude to someone who'd just returned a lost kid. While being kind to a Salinger wasn't her usual MO, there was a time and place for everything.

Lindsey was paranoid.

She had a long weekend to get unparanoid and butt out of Rundle business, because Zach had a job to get back to.

CHAPTER FOUR

THE THREE SALINGER SISTERS together in one room was a good sign that something wasn't normal. Middle sister Savannah rarely showed her face around their dad's. Her two kids and her husband kept her running, or so she said. Katie, the youngest, was in her last semester at the University of Kansas and had more friends and dates than Lindsey had arm hairs. She made it home when she could but being a social goddess took a lot of time.

As it happened, they'd all shown up Sunday afternoon to check on their dad and had been easily convinced by Mrs. Hale, who might as well have been a member of the family, to stay for dinner.

Lindsey hopped up to help serve homemade angel food cake with strawberries for dessert. Savannah's kids, Allie and Logan, had already escaped to the basement to play Tarzan—or something equally loud. Lindsey had considered joining them but opted to spend time with her sisters while she could. Katie was heading back later tonight.

"Anyone need a refill yet? It's decaf." Mrs. Hale carried the coffeepot to the table.

"I need the real stuff," Katie said. "I have a test in media law tomorrow."

"Let me guess," Savannah said. "You haven't started studying yet."

Katie grinned and pushed her hair off her forehead. "You got it. Too much going on."

"She'll ace it," Lindsey said. "She always does."

"Someone had to get the brains in the family," Michael piped up.

Savannah frowned at her husband then turned back to Katie. "Our favorite smart-ass."

"Jealous?" Katie asked.

"Hardly. Linds, are you still coming to the winter carnival next weekend?"

"Unless you let me off kitchen duty," Lindsey said. "What about you, Katie? Going to make it back?"

"When is it?"

"Saturday. Starts at noon and goes on all day."

Katie shook her head. "Got a date."

"Who's the lucky guy?"

"Just a guy," Katie said in a bored voice. "No one to get your panties in a knot about."

Everyone laughed except their dad.

"What's got you so grumpy?" Lindsey asked him.

"He's still ticked off about the newspaper," Katie said. "Right, Daddy?"

"Hell. Boneheads."

"Don't go getting your blood pressure up, Wendell." Mrs. Hale gave him her mild version of the evil eye. It was tough for a plump, matronly woman to carry off.

The newspaper in question was the *Lone Oak Leader,* their dad's weekly. He was the editor and it was as much his baby as the three sisters were. His work was everything. It was making him crazy to take time off to recuperate.

"I promise you very few people are going to know the mayor was misquoted on page six last week. You apologized. He accepted. Try to forget about it," Katie said.

"They should never have run the ice-skating story on page one. Mary knows better than that. I'm going in for the final edit this week."

"No, you're not," Lindsey and Mrs. Hale said at the same time.

Katie laughed. "Guess you're not, Daddy."

He was muttering what he thought of their overprotectiveness when the doorbell chimed. Lindsey got up to answer it.

She wasn't in the habit of using the peephole, so she was more than a little surprised to see Zach when she opened the door.

"Uh, hi," she said through the screen door. She looked over her shoulder to see if anyone in the kitchen had noticed who their visitor was. Cheerful conversation, so she figured she was safe.

"I need to talk to you," Zach said.

"And here I thought maybe you

brought me a thank-you present for bringing your grandma's possible health problems to light."

When he focused those eyes on her, she tried hard not to be affected.

"My grandma doesn't have health problems."

Lindsey stepped outside and eased the screen door closed behind her. Crossing her arms, she said, "This better be important. I don't want my dad to see you here."

"He'll be fine."

"He just had heart surgery. I don't want you upsetting him." She glanced nervously over her shoulder again. "Back to your grandma's health."

"I've been with her for three days now. My grandma is fine."

She raised an eyebrow.

"What, exactly, do you think is wrong with her?" In spite of his obvious agitation, she read concern in his dark brown eyes.

That concern, of course, got to Lindsey in spite of herself, in spite of everything. He wasn't as bad as he wanted everyone to believe. Why couldn't she remain cold and unfeeling with this guy?

"I'm not trying to cause trouble. She just wasn't herself the other night when I took Owen back."

"You said she was friendly. That's not a crime."

She shoved her hands into the back pockets of her jeans, frustrated. "No. Not a crime. But definitely unprecedented."

"She told me she was grateful you'd returned Owen. Seems like a good enough reason to me."

"Could be. But I swear she didn't know me from Eve. She acted disoriented. Confused. Maybe I'm overreacting but my instincts are usually right on. The other night they told me something was wrong."

"I haven't noticed any confusion."

Lindsey tried hard to see the situation from his perspective. It was natural for him to want to give his grandma the benefit of the doubt. "I'm not an expert, but some of the first signs of dementia are not recognizing people, forgetting things."

He ran one hand along his stubble-covered, hard-angled jaw. "I don't like where you're going with this."

"Where am I going?"

"Labeling her based on one encounter. She *isn't* demented."

This was getting nowhere and her dad was too close. "Zach, why are you here?"

He leaned back against the sturdy wooden railing, and she couldn't help noticing how well his worn jeans hugged his muscular thighs.

"I'm taking off for Wichita tomorrow. I came to tell you to leave my grandma alone."

"To tell me or to threaten me?"

"It's none of your business what goes on in that house." He indicated the yellow Victorian with a nod of his head.

"I'm worried about Owen."

"What do you think she's going to do to him? Beat him? Lock him in the basement?"

Lindsey took a deep breath. "I don't think she would intentionally hurt him. I could see she cares about him when I took him home. Otherwise I wouldn't have left him with her."

"What'll it take to get you to drop it?"

She crossed her arms again. "For me to

drop it?" She met his challenging gaze and didn't back down. "Take care of Owen yourself."

"I can't do that. I have a job to get back to."

"Then prepare to have me on neighborhood watch."

His eyes narrowed as he sized her up, and then he gave a halfhearted chuckle. She couldn't tell if he was angry or amused, but it didn't matter.

"Lindsey?" Wendell's voice reached from the other side of the screen door.

Uh-oh.

"He's leaving, Dad. Go sit down. I'll take care of it."

Zach glanced from her to her father and back again. "Watch all you want. Just do it from a distance."

He turned and walked down the front steps at a leisurely pace, driving home the point that he couldn't be forced away unless he was ready to go. Whatever. As long as he went.

She opened the door and waited for her dad to step out of her way. A muscle in his jaw twitched.

"The kid again?" His voice was deceptively calm. Didn't go with the look in his eyes at all.

She walked past him, heading for the kitchen. "Come on, Dad. Don't worry about it. Please sit down and relax."

"Wish I could," he muttered.

They were at the doorway to the kitchen now, and everyone was staring at them.

"What's wrong?" Mrs. Hale's eyebrows dipped in concern.

"Zach Rundle was at the door."

"Why?" Savannah didn't seem overly interested, but then that was her way.

Katie fixed Lindsey with a suspicious glare.

"I don't trust that family to make sure a five-year-old boy is taken care of properly," Lindsey answered defensively. She tried to direct her dad back to the table, but he pulled his arm away. Then he shuffled to his chair and sat down anyway.

Guilt gnawed at her. She knew her dad was upset—much more than he showed. She wished she could let it go, stop worrying about Owen.

Katie's chair scraped against the old

vinyl floor as she stood. "Time for me to fly."

Lindsey could have kissed her for the distraction, even though she sensed there was something her little sister wasn't saying. Katie wouldn't look directly at her.

The kitchen became a jumble of activity as everyone cleared the table and Katie got ready to leave for Lawrence.

Katie bent to kiss their dad on the forehead, then she turned to Lindsey. "Watch yourself."

Usually Lindsey was the one giving Katie advice. "Good luck on the test," was all she could think to say.

"She doesn't need luck," Michael said, winking at Katie.

Katie went to the sink where Savannah was scraping dishes and wound her arms around her sister from behind, then turned and hugged Michael, who stood near the door.

"Drive safe," their dad hollered as she rushed out the back door.

"We need to go, too, Savannah," Michael said.

Without looking at him, Savannah

called the kids up from the basement, to a duo of protests. After a good five minutes of debates and getting their coats on, the four of them headed out to the car.

"Talk to you soon," Lindsey said at the back door.

"Not so quick," Savannah replied. "Kids, go get in the car. I'll be right there." Michael was already climbing into the driver's seat.

"Bye, Aunt Lindsey!"

"Bye, guys! Where's my hug?"

Logan, who was four, ran toward her and grasped Lindsey's leg. Allie, seven, moved slower and made a lot less noise as she wrapped her arms around Lindsey's waist. As they pranced off to the minivan, Allie scolded Logan for not zipping his coat.

Lindsey smiled, then turned to her sister. "What's up?" *As if she didn't know.*

"Why are you talking to Zach Rundle?"

"I'm not. He's gone. Can we drop it?"

"What does Josh have to say for himself? Isn't it his kid?"

"Josh is gone. That's the problem, or part of it."

"I wouldn't say getting rid of Josh Rundle is a problem."

"For you and me it's a blessing. But maybe not for his son."

"I could argue that."

"Point taken. But I don't think that woman is up to caring for a child."

"It's not your problem, Linds."

"It's Owen's problem. And who's going to stick up for him if his family doesn't?"

Savannah studied her. She shook her head slowly and started toward the van. Lindsey walked with her.

"I know better than to think I can talk you out of it."

"Good," Lindsey said. "Then don't say anything else."

Savannah stopped. "If you're going to keep tabs on the Rundles, keep it to yourself. Dad will never accept it." Savannah stared at her for several seconds, then turned to get in the van. "Be careful. They've hurt our family enough."

Lindsey was fully aware Josh had turned their lives upside down. She was at the heart of it all—the pain, the guilt. No one needed to lecture her on it.

She saw the wisdom in Savannah's advice, though. She planned to make sure Owen was safe without letting her dad know a thing about it.

CLAUDIA HALE SHUT THE DOOR after Lindsey left, locking it for the night. At the table, Wendell sat quietly fuming.

"Well?" she said.

He glanced at her, a scowl deepening the wrinkles on his face. "Well, what?"

"You're upset."

"Yes, I'm upset. Are you surprised?"

"Surprised? No." It'd been years and he still reacted to the Rundles the same way. "Worried? Yes."

"How can she stand to talk to those people?"

"You know how she is, Wendell. Girl's heart is bigger than a house. Wouldn't want her any other way."

"Those people are bad news. I don't want them to hurt my family anymore." His volume hadn't risen, but strong feeling emphasized every word.

"You need to get a hold on your anger toward the neighbors—"

"They killed my wife."

"One man killed your wife. The rest of the family had nothing to do with it."

"Maybe if they weren't so dysfunctional, that kid wouldn't have been driving drunk that night."

Maybe, but who knew? "You have to stop blaming the family, especially now that Lindsey is getting involved."

"How about if she just doesn't get involved?"

"Take a deep breath and calm down." She took the seat next to him and put her hand on his. "Please. This anger is eating you up."

He only growled.

Claudia pulled her hand away. She didn't want to push him too far because he was too riled as it was. But some things needed to be said. "If it was any other child you'd be proud of her. This is who she is. This is Elizabeth coming out in her. And it's why you loved your wife so much."

He leaned back in his chair. "I worry about her. They're not the kind of people I want her to mess around with."

"She's just trying to help the boy. She doesn't mean to hurt you. She's the best daughter you could ask for."

If she'd had any children of her own, she'd have loved for them all to be as caring as Lindsey, although she definitely wouldn't want them to be as tormented. Claudia had long suspected Lindsey harbored guilt about her mother's accident. Lindsey never said anything about it. In fact, she refused to talk about the accident or her mom.

"I know she is. Guess that's why I don't understand her burning need to meddle with them."

At least his scowl was gone. She cared about him so much; she wouldn't be able to stand it if he had another heart attack.

"You better work on not letting the Rundles get to you so much. I have a hunch this isn't going to be resolved tomorrow."

Time to drop the subject and do what she did best—take care of Wendell. And if her niggling feelings were on target, he was going to need an extra dose of nurturing in the coming days.

"I DON'T WANNA GO TO bed yet," Owen said.

Zach had to hide a chuckle when he saw the don't-play-games-with-me look his grandma gave his nephew across the kitchen table.

"Get going. Uncle Zach will be up in a few minutes to make sure you've brushed your teeth."

Owen slid down from the wooden chair where he'd just finished his bedtime snack and scurried across the room.

"He's more comfortable with you," Zach said quietly as Owen headed up the stairs. He hated that she volunteered him to play dad.

"You need to lighten up with the boy," his grandma said. "Have fun with him. He won't bite."

"Fun?" He stood and walked to the kitchen counter to dump the rest of his Coke down the sink.

Kids weren't fun. They were small people who needed a lot from big people. They *deserved* a lot from them. But sometimes adults weren't capable of giving kids what they needed. He'd found that out after his dad died and his mom had had better things to do.

Zach was about as qualified to take care of Owen as a carpenter ant was to build a five-story office building.

A loud thud just outside the kitchen in the backyard made him glance at his grandma. But her widened eyes said she didn't know what it was anymore than he did.

He turned out the overhead light, leaving the kitchen shadowed and dim. Glancing out the back door, he saw movement in the yard.

"Make you a deal. You check on Owen. I'll go investigate."

"Don't be foolish, Zachary. If someone's out there, stay inside."

"I'm a big boy, Gram. Go check on the kid."

As soon as she was out of sight, he grabbed a set of keys from a kitchen drawer, then slipped into the formal dining room they never used. He still knew which key opened the drawer of the buffet. He took out Gram's gun and slid the drawer closed without a sound.

Back in the kitchen, he looked out the

window again. He thought he spotted someone disappearing behind the corner of the converted in-law quarters that stood halfway to the back property line.

Easing the door open, he listened carefully, but heard nothing in the frosty night. He crept down the stairs and into the shadow of the shop. About two feet from the end of the wall he stopped, straining to listen.

Seconds ticked by. Zach sensed someone was there, so he remained still, waiting. Barely breathing. Then he heard a rough, scraping noise against the stone exterior of the building, and his heart raced with adrenaline.

"Move another inch and I'll shoot you," he said in a low voice, holding the gun in front of him.

CHAPTER FIVE

"CHRIST, ZACH, GIMME a break."

Zach knew the slurred, intoxicated voice immediately. He swore under his breath and lowered the gun, putting the safety back on, and took two long steps around the corner.

His brother squatted there, his back against the wall for support. The urge to knock Josh in the head made his fingers itch. He didn't see his brother much, but Josh was drunk more than he was sober as far as Zach could tell. A total waste. He could be so much more. Like a father, for instance.

"What are you doing here?"

"I live here." Josh didn't move, didn't look up.

"Could've fooled me. If you live here, get your ass inside and take care of your son."

Josh spit into the grass in front of him. "Can't." He shrugged, and Zach clenched his hand into a fist.

"Why the hell not? He's your responsibility."

"Grandma takes care of him better 'n I could."

"What does a five-year-old want with an eighty-year-old woman taking care of him? You think she's going to run around with him in the yard?"

Zach almost choked on his own self-righteousness, as if he had a clue what a five-year-old kid needed.

"Save your breath, Zach. I ain't coming back."

"Looks to me like you're back."

"I just wanted to see him for a second." He shook his head. "Still can't believe that boy in there came from me."

"Neither can I." Zach wasn't in the mood for gushing about the wonder of it all. "You think Grandma's going to be around until he's eighteen?"

Josh had the nerve to laugh. "That old woman's too tough to die. She'll kick death in the ass when it comes after her."

"Owen isn't her job." Zach slid the gun under his waistband. He lodged his foot a couple feet up the stone wall and leaned on his bent knee. "She's already paid her dues bringing up two hell-raising generations of us."

Several seconds passed before Josh answered. "I ain't cut out to be a dad, no matter how bad I want to."

The words sliced through Zach's anger. He'd had identical thoughts about himself not fifteen minutes ago. Neither one of them knew what a good parent or a normal family was.

Still, someone had to try.

"So you're just going to get skunked and spy on your son when the mood suits you?"

Josh shrugged. "I didn't plan on comin' here. I just wanted to see him."

"Where you staying?"

"Around."

"Around where?"

Josh stood slowly, using the wall to steady himself. "None of your business."

"Get off the property."

Josh met his eyes then, narrowing his

own as if to gauge whether Zach was serious.

"I mean it."

They stared at each other for close to a full minute before Josh spit again, muttered an obscenity and set out on his unsteady way. He sauntered away from the shop and the house, across the barren field.

Zach watched him for as far as he could see him. When different shades of blackness started playing with his eyes, making him unsure whether it was Josh he saw or just more darkness, he turned away.

He shouldn't have let his temper get the best of him. Josh needed encouragement. The world gave him nothing but a cold shoulder. He deserved more from his own brother.

What was he doing sending Josh away instead of dragging him inside?

Zach went into the house, locked the gun back in the drawer and went upstairs to find his grandma. She was reading to Owen in Zach's old twin bed with the familiar red-and-blue bedspread. He reminded himself—not for the first time—that the guest room suited Zach just fine. He wasn't staying.

"Grandma's reading a story," Owen told him.

"I see that." Zach smiled.

"Stay and listen. Please?"

Zach didn't really have time to hear the resolution of *The Little Engine That Could,* but he sat on the edge of the bed and focused on his grandma's gravelly voice, wondering when she'd started getting so old.

Owen was hanging on her every word. Zach himself had been too old for stories by the time Gram had taken them in—or at least he'd thought he was.

He was just fine now, no matter how his childhood had been. And a lot of that was thanks to the bony, white-haired woman making *choo-choo* noises for all she was worth.

When the story was over, he bent toward Owen. "Night, O." He held out his fist and Owen punched it softly as Zach had taught him to the night before.

"G'night, Uncle Zach."

Zach wandered out to the hall to wait

for his grandma. "Josh was out back," he said as she shut Owen's door.

She looked around, clearly pleased.

"He ran off. Staggered, actually."

"You didn't go after him?"

"I'll go and see if I can find him. Shouldn't be too hard."

She nodded, worry wrinkling her forehead. "You think he'll come home?"

"I'll do what I can to get him here."

"Don't hurt him, Zachary," she hollered after him as he jogged downstairs. "Just bring him home."

Zach went out to his truck. He'd bet money Josh had headed over to County Road Nine, which was about a mile from their backyard on the other side of two fields.

He felt sure if he hurried he'd find Josh's old blue truck parked along the side of the road somewhere, maybe in a grove of trees, but probably right out in the open. Josh wasn't careful, but he was predictable. He made the same mistakes over and over, and that was why Zach guessed his brother was out driving under the influence, without a thought to the woman he'd killed doing exactly that nearly thirteen years ago.

It was time to turn that pattern around, get his brother help.

He turned right on Walnut and sped toward Nine.

LINDSEY WAITED UNTIL SHE WAS in bed, curled up in her oversized Astros jersey, to dial Katie's cell phone.

"Yeah?" Katie answered curtly. She must've seen it was Lindsey on her caller ID. Lindsey's suspicion that something was bugging her must be correct.

"Are you home yet?"

"I'm studying at the donut shop. What's wrong?"

"I was just making sure you got back okay."

"I did."

"Katie, you're pissed. I can tell."

She heard a sigh over the line. "I'm not pissed, Linds. I just don't understand how you can even look at those people without thinking about Mom and what they did."

"*Josh* did. Not 'they.'"

She'd long ago learned to turn off her

emotions when she needed to. Except her contempt for Josh. She wished she could turn off the nagging attraction for Zach while she was at it, but even tonight, she couldn't help thinking about running her fingers through his dark hair, tasting his lips again....

God. Enough already.

"It's Josh's kid, right?"

"He's gone, Katie." Lindsey explained what was going on next door.

"So the old hag is losing it?"

"I don't know. What would you think if she smiled at you and acted friendly?"

"I'd think she was smoking some really strong stuff."

"My thoughts exactly."

"I'm not saying I agree with what you're doing. You need to butt out unless it's bad enough to get involved professionally."

"I don't want it to get that far. He's a sweet kid."

"You're as stubborn as Savannah in your own special way."

"Gee, thanks. Love you, too."

"Linds? Is Dad really okay?"

"From what the doctors tell me, yeah."

"He didn't look okay when I left."

"Of course he didn't. He was seething over Zach's visit."

"You can't do that to him!"

"I don't intend to," Lindsey said, sweat beginning to bead on her forehead. What was it with her sisters? She was the one who was there for their dad every day, had visited him in the hospital twice a day. *She* was the one he relied on. Had been ever since the accident.

"I have to go. I have a lot of studying to do."

"I'll talk to you later." Lindsey sighed as she hung up.

She set the phone on her nightstand and flicked off the lamp. Pressure built in her chest. Didn't it just figure the Rundles were still causing problems for her family?

ZACH HAD SCOURED the nooks and crannies of the county road, even taken a couple of the dirt side roads that led nowhere.

Nothing.

Josh was gone. There was no sign of his rusting, blue Chevy anywhere.

Not more than ten minutes had passed from the time he'd watched Josh walk away to the time Zach had headed back outside to track him down. A healthy guy could run to the county road in that time, but Josh was drunk. The only exercise he got was running from trouble. There was no way he'd made it to the road before Zach.

He'd have to find him. Apologize. Convince him to come home and be a dad. He'd have to wait till daylight, though.

The neon sign in the window of one of the two taverns in Lone Oak beckoned to him as he drove. He hadn't been in the Lazy Goat in years, but he found himself pulling into the gravel lot beside it.

Josh might've stopped here to bolster his confidence. All he had to do was go north through the field instead of east. Downtown Lone Oak, such as it was, was only a couple of long residential blocks from the field and their backyard.

Zach sucked in a breath before opening the door to the tavern. Just as he expected, when he took a step inside, all heads turned his way. The good news was there weren't many people there at ten o'clock on a Sunday night.

He glanced over the dark, smoky interior, searching for Josh.

Not much had changed in the years since he'd been there—if anything. A pool table and a dartboard crowded one back corner. Two older men looked to be in the middle of a cutthroat game of pool. A handful of mismatched tables were occupied. At the far end of the bar a man and a woman looked like they could use a hotel room. But there was no sign of his brother.

Zach made a path toward the unoccupied end of the bar, where the female bartender looked him over, waiting for his drink order.

"Zach Rundle," the short woman said slowly.

He studied her more carefully, trying to come up with a name. Her face was familiar but he couldn't place her. He slid onto a stool, not overjoyed at being in a place where everyone knew his name.

"What'll you have?"

Glancing at the tap, he saw his brand and ordered a draught.

"You don't know who I am, do you?" the woman asked as she filled a mug.

"You're familiar."

"If you'd'a showed up for school more than once a week you might remember. Heather."

He nodded as he set a five on the bar. "Heather Casper. I remember fine."

"Rawlins, actually. Haven't been Casper for a long time."

"Married?"

"Divorced. You?"

"Single. Liking it that way."

She raised an arched eyebrow to tell him she wasn't interested in him, anyway.

"You know my brother Josh?"

"Know him well."

"He been in here tonight?"

"Haven't seen him for a while," she said as she wiped down the bar.

"How often does he come in?"

"Used to be nearly every night, but he hasn't been in for over a week as far as I know."

So he wasn't getting his liquor here. Ellington and Layton were only ten miles down the road in different directions. Josh must be avoiding people who knew him.

Heather emerged from behind the bar and headed to the noisy table in the front corner. Zach took a swallow of beer and considered his options.

The way he saw it, he could leave tomorrow as he'd planned, go back to Wichita and make the commission meeting tomorrow night to fight for the zoning change. He was just about ticked off enough at Josh to walk away, to let him screw up his life some more.

Just about.

Or he could stick around and track down Josh. If he didn't find him tomorrow, he could zip down to Wichita for the meeting and come back Tuesday to resume his search.

He had to try. Josh needed a shove in the right direction.

Zach would do what he could to get Josh back home with Owen, to get them help. There had to be some kind of classes or programs for single fathers. And help for the drinking. Josh could probably still get his old job back. Gram would be there as backup, he had a place to live for free… Josh could do this.

Then Zach could go back to Wichita for good, back to the drama-free existence he appreciated more each day. Peace at last.

Heather was back behind the bar, looking at a man a few feet from Zach.

"Hey, Humph. What're you doing out on a Sunday?"

Kurt Humphrey. He hadn't changed much since ninth grade, when he and Zach had fought in the gravel lot behind the school. Zach couldn't remember why now.

"Looking for you, darlin'."

"As if." Heather smiled. She flipped a cardboard coaster on the bar, drew a beer without asking what kind, and set it in front of him.

Zach didn't care to watch her flirt, and he had nothing to say to Humphrey so he stared at the swirled grain of the ancient wood under his drink. He felt Humphrey looking his way and tensed. He wasn't up for a confrontation.

But Humphrey ambled off to the table he shared with two others. When Zach turned to see if he recognized either of them, he met three sets of eyes.

"Assholes," he muttered to himself as he turned back toward the bar.

"Who? Humph and company?" Heather was closer than he'd thought, mopping off the bar. "What'd they do to you?"

"Don't worry about it."

"They're decent, unlike a lot we get in here."

"Regular saints." The good guys. As opposed to the Rundles.

Heather crossed her arms over her chest and leaned on the bar in front of Zach, studying him.

"What?" he asked.

"You've changed."

He chuckled, not actually finding anything funny. "You don't know me. Never did."

"No, but I know people. I spend six nights a week dealing with all kinds. You still brood, but you're different. Not so pissed at the world."

"Amazing what getting out of this town

does for a guy." He pushed his beer mug, only half-empty, toward her and stood.

"Going home so soon? We're just starting to get along." Heather winked.

Zach smiled. She was blunt, but he didn't mind her. "See you later," he said, even though he wouldn't.

His short time in this dump had reminded him of why he'd better find Josh fast. How long could it take to track down a drunk in a fifteen-year-old truck?

CHAPTER SIX

THERE WEREN'T ENOUGH HOURS in the day, and there sure weren't enough good people out there willing to adopt older children who'd lost their homes.

Lindsey walked into her office after a depressing morning. First she'd met with a boy at the middle school, along with the guidance counselor and his dad. The dad was bad news. It'd only be a matter of time before they had to get the kid away from his father if Lindsey's hunch was right. She hoped she was wrong but her instincts were fairly reliable.

Then she'd visited Billy, the six-year-old who'd just been placed in the group home two days ago. He should've been in first grade this school year, but it turned out his mother didn't think school was too important. Apparently she'd left him by himself regularly. For days on end. She'd scare him to death before she left, threatening to beat him if he set foot outside. Then she'd come home and beat him anyway, judging by the marks on the boy's body.

Lindsey sat down slowly at her desk, her heart heavy. As was usually the case, it was a good thing to get this child out of his home, away from the people who hurt him in so many ways. The group home was a decent place. She knew the women who ran it, knew most of the employees and volunteers. They were decent, caring people.

But it still wasn't family, and visiting always made Lindsey sad.

Billy was still so innocent considering what he'd been through. She wanted to find a permanent home for him before he became withdrawn or jaded. Before he lost hope of belonging to a family.

Lindsey glanced at the clock on her desk and did a double take when she saw it was time to meet Brooke down the street for a late lunch.

Setting Billy's file on top, she shoved

her papers into something resembling stacks and grabbed her long coat from the hook on the wall. She'd have to make it a quick lunch; otherwise she'd be working till midnight.

LINDSEY STEPPED INTO Tuttle's Diner—known locally as Tut's—and waited for her eyes to adjust. Windows ran around the perimeter of the restaurant, but blinds had been pulled down to keep the sun out of diners' eyes. She knew her friend was already here—Brooke excelled at the science of being early.

Brooke waved from a dark-green upholstered booth along the far left wall.

"Been waiting long?" Lindsey asked as she slid into the seat.

"Not too. I was on hold for eons with one of my suppliers." She stuck her cell phone into her jute purse.

Jane came up to the table at that moment. The fifty-something waitress had worked there as long as Lindsey could remember and knew their preferences just about better than they did. "Monday special and a salad?"

They both nodded.

"Bring your own dressing?" Jane asked Brooke.

"Of course." She opened her bag and took out a small plastic container. None of that unhealthy mass-produced dressing for her.

"So how was dinner at Dad's last night?" Brooke asked.

"Typical Salinger fare. A fly-by from Katie. Lecture from Savannah. Disagreement with Dad."

"Ooh, you were all there. Details, please."

"You should've stayed up if you wanted to know so bad," Lindsey teased her.

"Hmm, Salinger scoop or bed. Tough one."

They'd lived together ever since college. Brooke had no family in town so she liked to keep up with Lindsey's. Only from afar, though. She rarely joined Lindsey for family stuff even though she was regularly invited. Brooke didn't dislike people, she just preferred being by herself eighty percent of the time.

"So the whole family was there?"

"Yeah. Wasn't planned, but it reeked of a mini-holiday get-together. Didn't end quite so festive, though."

"Let me guess. Savannah and your dad got into it again."

"Nope. This time it was the good daughter upsetting Dad."

Jane stuck plates of food in front of them, and Lindsey flipped her bun off to make sure there was no mustard.

"What'd you do to dear ol' dad?"

Lindsey took a bite, chewed and swallowed it before answering. "He found me on the front porch talking to the enemy."

Brooke's eyes widened.

"Zach Rundle."

Her friend put her fork down on the table. "What was that bad boy doing on your dad's front porch?"

"Trying to get me to forget about his nephew."

"What are you doing to his nephew now?"

"Nothing yet. But I intend to keep an eye on him. Make sure the old bat is capable of caring for him."

"You really think she isn't?"

Lindsey shrugged. "All I know is that a five-year-old boy shouldn't be wandering around outside in the cold. At night. By himself."

"It could've been an honest slipup."

"Could've been."

Brooke shoved a bite of salad into her mouth and looked thoughtful as she chewed, "What are you going to do?"

Lindsey expelled a frustrated sigh. "Whatever I can."

"Can you open a case on him?"

Lindsey made a snortlike *hmph.* "I wish. Not that I want him in the system, but it would be easier to make sure everything's okay if I could."

"Why can't you?"

"There's not enough. Ever since the state hacked the budget, our hands are tied until there's obvious abuse or neglect."

"I'd call a boy out wandering around without shoes neglect."

"You would. And I would. But the agency can't. Besides, even if I had a legitimate case, they'd say I'm too close to it to work on it."

"But at least someone could get in there and see what's going on."

Lindsey nodded, setting her burger down. Her appetite had taken a hike. "So. We're back to me keeping an unofficial eye on Owen. That should be easier since Zach left for Wichita today."

Even though she felt Owen was safer with Zach home, she didn't like coming into contact with him. She couldn't help but worry her dad would go into cardiac arrest again.

"Well, if it isn't the devil himself," Brooke said as she tossed her napkin onto her empty plate.

Lindsey followed Brooke's stare. Zach walked toward the counter along the back wall, focused on his destination. However, Lindsey noticed several sets of eyes following him. The Rundle brothers had always been able to cause a stir when they showed up somewhere.

"I thought he was gone," Lindsey said, mostly to herself.

"I'd say not. And he can darken our front porch any day." Brooke grinned at Lindsey, flipped a ten on the table, and stood. "I need to get back to it. See you tonight."

Lindsey didn't respond. She absently stuck a French fry in her mouth, then realized it was cold and tasteless.

Brooke was the only person who knew about Lindsey's ill-advised tryst with Zach back in high school, and now Lindsey wished she hadn't told even her.

She gestured to Jane for the bill. Zach was ordering takeout at the counter and hadn't noticed her.

She fumbled in her purse to get her cash ready for a quick escape. When she looked up again, Zach stood inches away from her.

"Hello, neighbor," she said with forced cheer.

"Mind if I sit for a minute?"

He wore an old pair of jeans and a lined flannel shirt. Everyday work clothes for him, she assumed. Yet his presence was as compelling as any businessman dressed in tailored slacks and a tie. The complexity in him intrigued her.

Several people were watching them, so she motioned for him to sit across from her, hoping that would generate less attention. He eased into the booth, his legs brushing her knees in the process.

"You're supposed to be gone," Lindsey said, checking around the restaurant again to see exactly who had spotted them together.

"I'm not. Happy to see me?"

"Did you come to threaten me some more?"

The waitress slipped Lindsey the check and a puzzled look, but kept on walking.

He shook his head. "Just a question. Have you seen my brother lately?"

"No," she said abruptly. "I haven't been looking for him."

"Fair enough." He picked up the unused spoon in front of him and spun it around. "What are you so nervous about?"

"I'm not."

"You keep looking over your shoulder." So she did.

"Don't want to be seen with me, huh?" He almost sounded like he was kidding, but there was an edge to his tone.

"I don't want my dad hearing about it is all."

Zach leveled a stare at her that made her uncomfortable.

"If you do happen to see my brother, could you call me?"

"I can't promise I won't run him down."

"I found him out back last night. I'm going to get him home."

"Why?" She didn't care if her horror showed on her face.

"To take care of Owen."

It took a gargantuan effort for Lindsey not to comment.

"He cares about the kid. I could tell last night."

"I thought your grandma was just fine to take care of Owen."

"She is." His grumpiness had returned, if it'd ever left. "But Owen needs his dad. It'd do Josh a world of good, too. He needs a reason to get his act together."

This was exactly why she'd never be able to work with the Rundles if it ever rose to case status. Fundamentally, Lindsey believed people like Josh deserved a chance, as long as the child wasn't endangered. Sometimes all people needed were support and resources. Someone who believed in them.

But she would never, ever believe in Josh. Her distrust and hatred for him were so deeply ingrained, she couldn't be impartial.

Personally she wanted to make sure Owen stayed far, far away from his biological father. But professionally, she realized they deserved a chance to make it work.

She didn't feel the need to tell Zach that, though. If he wanted to get his hopes up for Josh, that was his problem.

"Well?" he asked.

"Since when do you look for my approval?"

"It wasn't your approval I wanted. I figured you'd have something to say. You always do." He met her eyes, his expression…amused? He tapped the end of the spoon on the table once.

"Owen doesn't have any good options. Grandma's old, at the very least. Josh is allergic to responsibility and is an alcoholic. Finding another home for a child is never my first choice."

Zach rubbed a hand over his face and sighed. "What would you do if you were in my shoes?"

Why on earth did she actually wish she could help him?

"I don't know, but I doubt it would involve your brother."

"You'll never forgive him, will you?" Zach's expression seemed to soften.

"Have you?" she snapped without meaning to.

"Forgiven him?" He shrugged. "It's not the same. He's my brother. She wasn't my mother." He almost sounded apologetic.

Lindsey would rather have a dozen teeth pulled without anesthetic than continue this conversation. "I need to get back to work," she said, standing.

"Likewise," he said as he glanced at his watch. "Wichita calls."

He stood and walked to the counter as Lindsey turned toward the exit. Inez, the other waitress, was just putting his food in a plastic sack. She looked questioningly at Lindsey.

She wasn't the only one who wondered what the heck Lindsey was getting involved in. Word spread at the speed of light in this snail's pace town. Lindsey just hoped no one who'd seen her with Zach cared enough to mention it to her dad.

IT WAS AT TIMES LIKE THIS when Lindsey questioned her sanity.

She'd parked her car the next day half a block down and around the corner from her dad's house in a particularly shadowed area.

She was darn well going to find out if Mrs. Rundle was competent to care for Owen or if the way she'd acted the other night was the status quo. To make a judgment, she had to have some contact with the people, didn't she? The woman tended to hole up in her Victorian, and Lindsey rarely ran into her. Which was usually a good thing.

Mrs. Rundle would see through the cookies, Lindsey knew. No big deal. She wasn't trying to fool her so much as see if she recognized her this time. Beyond that, she didn't know what kind of oddness she was looking for. But getting inside, even for five minutes, would be a start.

Lindsey glanced toward her dad's house as she knocked.

Zach would give her grief if he found out she was "bothering" his family. She'd made sure his truck was gone before parking. He'd said he was leaving town yesterday afternoon but then she hadn't expected to run into him at Tut's, either.

The door opened slowly and she looked down at Owen peeking out at her. She smiled. "Hey, Owen, how are you?"

"Good! What's in there?" He stood on tiptoe to peer at the tin box she held.

"A surprise for you." Lindsey perused the hallway behind him. Seeing no one else, she bent down and took the lid off the box.

"Yummy! Chocolate chip?"

She nodded, but stopped when he started to grab for one. "Better make sure it's okay with your grandma first."

At that moment, Mrs. Rundle seemed to pop in out of nowhere, coming from the room behind the front door instead of from the hallway, as Lindsey had expected.

She saw Lindsey and frowned. "What are you doing here?"

Lindsey stepped over the threshold even though she wasn't invited. "Being nice to your grandson. He and I are buds, aren't we, Owen?" Yeah, she was playing it up for Mrs. Rundle's benefit. Pushing her, maybe.

"Can I have a cookie, Gram?"

Mrs. Rundle sneered as she examined the cookie tin. "You make those yourself?"

"I bought them at Sullivan's. They're safe," Lindsey said drily. The bakery at the only grocery store in town made irresistible cookies and pastries. No one could deny it, not even this critic.

Mrs. Rundle picked out two cookies and handed one to Owen. The other, she took a begrudging bite of. Lindsey hid a grin. She hadn't counted on making any points with the cranky woman, but maybe the cookies were one in her favor. Not that she wanted to be friends or anything.

The two ate their cookies in awkward silence. Under normal circumstances, Lindsey would bow out now and be on her way. But this wasn't normal. This was an info-gathering trip.

"So, Owen, do you go to school yet?"

He nodded, his mouth full of the last bite of cookie.

"Let me guess, kindergarten?"

"Yeah. Wanna see my totem pole?"

Before she could answer, he ran off, dropping crumbs on the faded olive-green carpet.

"I don't have the foggiest notion what you're trying to pull, but you're not welcome here."

"I didn't figure Owen had many friends. Not a lot of kids in the neighborhood anymore."

"And you think that's your business?"

"Just being friendly."

Mrs. Rundle looked her up and down suspiciously. "What's your daddy say about that?"

"You don't want to know," Lindsey said, nearly chuckling.

Owen ran back in and held out a paper towel tube he'd painted and glued with sets of wiggling eyes.

"You made that totem pole?" Lindsey asked. "I love it." She reached out for it and made a show of admiring it. "You're quite the artist."

"I know." He puffed up with pride. "I made it in school today." He ran off again, presumably to put the artwork back.

Mrs. Rundle nodded her head. "He needs friends. Someone other than an old lady. Owen?" she called. "Come tell this girl thank-you."

Owen zipped back in and said, "Thanks! Wanna play hide-and-seek again?"

"Maybe some other time. I need to check on my dad."

Before Lindsey could turn toward the door, Owen attached himself to her legs in a tight embrace. She bent, something unexpectedly tugging at her insides, and put her arms around him.

She said goodbye, but noticed Mrs. Rundle didn't thank her. However, the woman's face had softened a bit. Gone from scornful to begrudgingly blank. She'd done nothing during Lindsey's visit to signify any kind of memory problem, but then Lindsey didn't expect it would be easy to find evidence she was unwell. Zach had stayed with Mrs. Rundle all weekend and said he hadn't noticed anything wrong.

Lindsey still wasn't convinced, though.

As she walked to the driveway, a familiar black pickup truck drove up.

Busted.

Zach pulled up close to the single-car garage and turned off the engine. Lindsey had nothing to hide. So what if she'd gone against his warning from the other night? She'd told him she wasn't going to back down.

"Hello again," she said.

Zach stepped down from the truck and shut the door. His face was unreadable. "Thought I told you to stay away from my grandma."

"You did."

"Salinger, why do you insist on pissing me off?"

"It's too easy."

"What are you doing here?"

"I was visiting Owen."

He stared at her for a moment. "I guess that's better than the spying you did years ago."

"Spying?"

No way could he know she used to watch him work in his backyard shop at night. That was her secret. Something she hadn't even confessed to Brooke.

Now he did crack a grin, a smug one. "You think I didn't realize you sat out on your back porch and watched me?"

She didn't utter a word, didn't know what to say.

"Cat got your tongue, Salinger?"

"You're cocky, you know that?" Lame, she knew, but she wasn't about to fess up to spying.

She turned away, walked down the driveway. She felt his eyes on her back.

"You're going the wrong way," he called out when she turned the opposite direction from her dad's house on the sidewalk.

"I parked down there," she said over her shoulder, pointing at her Civic just visible at the end of the street.

"Ah, Daddy wouldn't approve of you paying a visit to the lowly neighbors, huh?"

She ignored him, walked to the car and drove the few hundred yards or so to her dad's.

Lindsey pulled as far into the driveway

as she could get, stopping behind Mrs. Hale's ancient VW Rabbit.

Her heart was still pounding double-time from the realization that all those years ago Zach had known.

CHAPTER SEVEN

ZACH FOUND GRAM AND Owen getting dinner ready when he came inside.

"What was Lindsey doing here?" he asked as he draped his jacket over the back of a chair.

Gram, who had just set a plate of burgers on the table, studied him as if she thought he knew more than he let on. The woman was way too *with it* for anyone's good. Lindsey was so far off base, it was almost laughable.

"She bringed me some cookies!" Owen said.

Zach looked to his grandma for confirmation. What the devil was she doing bringing cookies? Several distinct possibilities flooded his mind. Bribing Owen to be her friend, maybe give her the inside scoop over here. Getting inside the house to do her own twisted research. Doing the exact opposite of what Zach had warned her to do, to spite him. Or, okay, maybe she was just being nice.

"They're good cookies," Gram said.

"What, are you two friends now?"

His grandma laughed. "You know me better than that. But I do know cookies. Can't beat Sullivan's."

"Grandma said we could have another one after dinner."

"Let's get to it, then."

Dinner talk centered around safe topics, such as Owen's school day and what he'd built with Lego toys that afternoon. Once the plates were cleared, Owen gobbled up a cookie in record time, then Grandma sent him upstairs to get his pajamas on.

"Any luck finding that brother of yours today?" she asked after Owen had noisily clomped up the stairs.

Zach shook his head. "Not really." He munched on a pickle. "Stopped into a bar over in Ellington. The Rat's Nest. Seedy-looking place off behind the main drag. Talked to the manager there and he knows Josh. Said he'd been in recently for a drink."

"How recently?"

"He claims to not remember. Don't know if he's leveling with me or not. Anyway, I aim to check back there often."

"I hope he's okay."

"He might take some stupid risks, but he can take care of himself."

"He can do so much more than people give him credit for. They all wrote him off after the accident."

"Not totally without reason. Josh doesn't give himself enough credit half the time," Zach said as he took his plate to the counter, annoyed that Lindsey popped into his mind again. For twelve years now, ever since he'd come upon the accident scene, the image of Lindsey's anguish had been burned into his mind. Yesterday at the diner she'd shown him a flash of that same pain—when he'd brought up Josh. He wished like hell he could erase it for her.

Gram dipped her last bite of burger in the ketchup on her plate. "If you could get his butt back here at home... Being a daddy could change everything for him."

From his place at the counter, Zach

watched her take her last few bites of dinner. "Do you really believe that, Gram?" he finally asked.

She didn't blink an eye. "I do. Joshua has it in him. We just need to pull it out of him."

Zach nodded firmly once, glad to hear they were in agreement. There were moments he doubted his crusade to get Josh home, times when he wondered if he was crazy for thinking there was hope. But if Gram believed it, too, then they could help Josh work through his problems.

"The sooner we can start, the better. My boss called when I got back into Lone Oak today." Zach put the stopper in the sink and squeezed some dish soap under the running water.

"How did your meeting last night turn out, anyway?"

"Not good. The commission didn't go for the zone changes. Three of them didn't like our plan."

She walked to the counter and took charge of the dishes. "Now what?"

"Now we redraw the plans, change some of the stuff they objected to, try to keep the integral parts of what we want to create. Wouldn't be a huge deal if I was there to work on it. Chuck called to say he's having Adam French help."

"What's wrong with Adam French?"

"He's young, stupid and doesn't care about the company."

"So why's Chuck having him help?"

"So I can take care of business here, I imagine."

"Zachary, you need to get your buns back to Wichita and do your job. We can handle things just fine here."

He shook his head. "I need to get Josh home and get him on the right track first."

Keeping Lindsey out of Gram's hair was as big a part of his motivation as any, but he couldn't mention that.

"Well, for now, why don't you go up and—"

"I know, I know. Go see if Owen's getting ready for bed." He dried his hands and headed for the stairs. "I've got to get Josh back here just so you have someone else to boss around."

Gram's rough chuckle followed him up the stairs.

WHEN LINDSEY WALKED INTO her dad's kitchen, she was accosted by the to-die-for aroma of freshly baked coffee cake. Her dad and Mrs. Hale sat at the table, engrossed in a game of Scrabble.

"Mrs. Hale, you're spoiling him."

"Would you like some cake, dear? It's heart-healthy."

"I'll try some anyway. Hi, Dad."

He grunted as he set down his tiles to form a long word. "Don't talk to me when I'm concentrating. I aim to win this game."

"You're sixty-two points ahead, Wendell. I think it's in the bag," Mrs. Hale said as she cut a slice of cake.

"It's not over till it's over."

"I thought you hated playing Scrabble with him," Lindsey said.

"He was threatening to go in to work. It was the only way I could keep him home."

"Dad. You're not supposed to work yet. You're not supposed to drive, either. What are you thinking?"

"I'm thinking I'm going loony sitting around this house all the time. I was only going to look at the stories Mary's got lined up for tomorrow's paper."

"Uh-uh. You'd find something to edit. Or rewrite. Knowing you, you'd go out and track down the source and start from scratch on something. Not allowed."

He sighed. "What would I do without you two lovely ladies to run my life?"

"Have another heart attack, likely," Mrs. Hale stated matter-of-factly. She set a plate of cake and a glass of tea in front of Lindsey, then sat down to peruse her tiles.

"Killjoy." Her dad was actually a teddy bear under the layers of grump.

Before Mrs. Hale could form a word, the phone rang. Wendell picked up the cordless on top of a folded newspaper beside him.

"Hello." He listened for a moment, then handed the phone to Mrs. Hale.

She answered as she stood, and Lindsey caught the frown before the older woman took the phone to the living room for privacy.

"I'll fill in for her," Lindsey said, switching to the vacant chair.

"You think you can win for her, huh?"

"You got it."

She and her dad had always been cut-throat competitive at board games. They'd spent hours trash-talking over Scrabble and Trivial Pursuit when Lindsey had still lived at home.

She stared at the letters for a couple of minutes, then rearranged them. Her dad had left the triple word open, and she was going to capitalize on it. Somehow.

"I'm sorry I got so upset the other day, honey."

She looked at him. "No need to apologize. I'm sorry you found Zach here."

"I keep reminding myself you're just doing what you think is right."

She nodded. "I'm sorry that hurts you."

Lindsey's heart pounded guiltily. Had he seen her at the Rundles before she'd come over tonight? No, he'd been here at the table, engrossed in his match with Mrs. Hale. Maybe someone had ratted on her for sitting with Zach at Tut's.

"The boy is so innocent, Dad. I hate to think of him suffering in any way."

"Why can't they handle this boy on their own?"

"Because they're Rundles?" She smiled, relieved when her dad grinned. But at the same time, she felt like a traitor because she really liked Owen. Okay, maybe Zach, too. Against her better judgment.

She took his silence to mean the discussion was over and went back to her tiles.

Then she spotted it. Some quick calculations in her head had her grinning smugly. "Z-y-m-o-s-i-s." She named the letters as she laid them in place, something she'd always done when scoring big. It never failed to make her dad crazy.

"That's not a goddamn word."

"You challenging me?"

"Yes I am. Go get the dictionary."

She laughed as she jogged upstairs to Savannah's old room. The light in the hallway was on and was bright enough for her to see the bookcase on the opposite wall, so she didn't bother to turn on the bedroom light. After she picked out the dictionary, the adjacent bedroom in the Rundle house caught her eye.

Zach was carrying Owen over his shoulder like a sack of potatoes, horsing around. Lindsey moved closer to the window, surprised at his playfulness.

Zach pretended to throw the boy into bed and then the light in Owen's room went off. Lindsey was about to step away from the glass, when Zach's face appeared right in front of Owen's window. He stared straight at her in the darkness before pulling down the shade.

Oh, great. She wouldn't hear the end of this. Groaning, she hurried back downstairs with the dictionary.

Mrs. Hale was back at the table, tears in her eyes.

"What's going on?" Lindsey asked, setting the book aside, open to the page with her word on it.

"My sister, Ann, fell this afternoon. Broke her hip. She's going to have surgery tomorrow to replace it."

"Oh, I'm so sorry to hear that. How's she doing?"

"Pretty upset. Scared. But we'll get her through it. I told her I'd fly out and stay with her through the recovery." Mrs. Hale blew her nose. "I just hate to leave your dad by himself."

The look Mrs. Hale exchanged with her dad caught Lindsey by surprise. It went deep. Deeper than employer and employee, maybe even deeper than friends. The possibility that they might share more than she'd ever guessed stunned Lindsey.

"I'll be just fine, Claudia. I'm an adult."

"A stubborn, rule-breaking adult. I'll stay with him while you're gone," Lindsey said without hesitating. She absently jabbed her fork at her coffee cake.

"That'd certainly ease my mind."

"I don't need a babysitter."

"Yes, you do." Mrs. Hale put her hand over Wendell's. "Lindsey will keep an eye on you."

"How long will you be gone?" Lindsey asked.

"I don't know yet. A week or two. At least long enough to see her over the hump."

"Take however long you need."

"Thank you, dear."

Lindsey smiled. "The dessert patrol is here, reporting for duty."

"Just what I need. Two women ganging up on me," her dad said, grumpily.

"See, Dad, if you'd behaved yourself and followed the doctor's orders, you might have gotten some freedom now."

He narrowed his eyes.

"And by the way, *zymosis*. Right there." She held the dictionary out to him, pointing. "That's seventy-eight points, plus fifty for using all my tiles."

Her dad stared at her. Lindsey couldn't help cackling in victory as she stood to clear the dishes from the table. "Mrs. Hale, you take it from here."

Three hours later, Lindsey left her dad's and got into her car.

As soon as she cleared the house, a figure emerged from the shadows, causing her to slam on the brakes in surprise. Her heart was in her throat until she recognized the face outside her window as Zach's. She barely avoided the second Salinger heart attack in as many weeks.

Lindsey hit the power window button and lowered the glass halfway. "What are you *doing?*"

"Hey," Zach said nonchalantly. "You're out late tonight. Might as well move in with your old man."

She looked tired—her hair a mess, eyes hollow-looking in the dim light—but she looked as beautiful as he'd ever seen her.

"Funny you should mention it. I'm staying with him starting tomorrow."

"What? Is his health getting worse?" He wasn't sure how he felt about having her so close. Too much temptation.

"Just his attitude. The housekeeper has to go out of town."

"Guess that'll give you some extra time to spy," he said with a half grin. "You're getting sloppy with your undercover work, Salinger."

Instead of getting worked up like he expected her to, she smiled slowly. "Just can't keep myself from watching those troublemaker Rundles."

"Maybe I like knowing you're watching me."

His words got to her—he could tell when she wouldn't look directly at him.

"What are you doing here, anyway? If my dad sees you out here…"

"Hold on," he said, then jogged around the front of the car. As he opened the passenger door and climbed in, he noticed her checking the windows of the house nervously. Zach tried to ignore it. "I took my grandma to see Dr. Fletcher today."

Still glancing at the windows, Lindsey backed out of the driveway. "And?"

"Where are you taking me?" Zach made his voice lower, sexier than usual, infusing suggestiveness into the question.

"Don't get too excited." She pulled a few feet down the street, then turned into the Rundle driveway. "So, anyway. Grandma. Doctor. What happened?"

"She's one-hundred-percent fine."

"Did they run tests?" Her tone conveyed skepticism.

"Stress test, EKG, bunch of others. She's a normal eighty-year-old woman."

"That's debatable. What about mental tests? Or memory?"

"Don't think so. I guess the doctor didn't feel they were necessary."

"And you came over here to tell me this because…?"

"To put your mind at ease. I know how worried about my grandma you are."

"Cut the sarcasm. I'm worried about

Owen. So you think everything's fine then, huh?"

"I do."

"You still think she can keep up with a five-year-old?"

"As much as any of us can."

"What about long term, Zach? What happens when Grandma's eighty-five, ninety? Have you thought that far?"

"Josh will be back long before then."

When, exactly, Zach wasn't sure. Two full days of searching hadn't produced results. He was proving tougher to find than Zach had anticipated.

He reclined his seat a few inches and hooked his hands behind his head. When Lindsey didn't say a word, he glanced at her. She looked at him like he had a screw loose.

To hell with her. She didn't even know Josh.

She shook her head slowly.

"What?"

"You're living in some kind of alternate reality. Grandma has no problems. Josh will sober up and be a competent parent. Not a care in the world, right?"

"Look, I understand why you hate Josh so much. What I don't get is why you hate me."

Again, she wouldn't look at him. Didn't say a word, for once.

"Did you know that I came to your house to see you the night of your mom's funeral?"

Instant eye contact. There was no doubt she hadn't known. Not a big surprise.

"Your dad wouldn't let me in. Wouldn't even let you come to the door."

She stared at him for a long moment. "Why'd you do that?"

Good question. Better yet, why was he telling her now, when it couldn't matter less? And why did he have the most compelling urge to touch the smooth skin of her face, to reach across the small space between them and run his fingers along that jaw, which was normally so strongly set but which now seemed somehow fragile? She didn't want him. He needed to stop wanting her.

"Never mind." Gritting his teeth, he opened the door and got out, then leaned in. "Owen will be fine. Stop worrying about him."

"You know, there *is* an easy answer."

He waited, warily, for her cure-all.

"You could adopt Owen yourself."

"That's the worst idea I've heard in ages."

Lindsey shrugged. "You might want to move out of the way," she said. "I'm backing out now."

"Goodnight to you, too, sweetheart."

CHAPTER EIGHT

ELSA RUNDLE CLOSED HER bedroom door and leaned against it, breathing harder than she should be after just going up a flight of stairs. Fear did that to a person—stole the breath right out of you.

It'd happened again. She'd just wandered through the entire house trying to remember what it was she needed to do. There was something, she knew. But she sure couldn't recall what.

Some days she knew something was wrong with her. Other days she just figured she was older than sin and getting forgetful.

Forgetting scared the tar out of her. *Please Lord above, don't let me lose my mind.*

Nausea overcame her, and she shuffled to her bed. She lay down on her side on top of the bedspread, squeezing her eyes shut.

She still had no earthly idea what was so important that she had to do this morning.

Putting her hand to her chest, she could feel her heart thumping like a ground squirrel that had spotted a hawk.

Getting old was a daily wallop up the side of the head, but she wasn't ready to surrender to it yet. She still had plenty of fight left.

Feeling braver, she sat up on the edge of the bed, half expecting dizziness or the unsettling feeling of not quite remembering something. But there was nothing, just her familiar bedroom, with the antique dresser on the…

That was it. The stack of bills on the dresser. She was supposed to mail the things this morning. She'd drifted all over the house in a fog. What the living hell was wrong with her?

She lay down again, afraid to leave her room. She couldn't take Owen to the school carnival. What if she had a spell in public?

"Zachary!"

She heard his heavy footsteps clomping up the stairs and down the hall to her doorway. "Yeah, Gram, what's up?"

"I'm not feeling too well."

He entered her room and stood at the edge of her bed, concern etched into his face. "You getting sick?"

"Upset belly. I don't dare go more than twenty feet from the toilet, if you get my meaning."

The grimace on his face confirmed he did, thank goodness. Lying to him made her more than a little uncomfortable.

"Anything I can do?"

She was hoping he'd ask. "I promised Owen I'd take him to that carnival at the school." She paused. "I don't want to let him down."

"Does he know it's today?"

"Oh, yes. Haven't you heard him going on about it?"

Zach crossed his arms and looked at the ceiling. "You want me to take him."

"I hate to think of him missing it."

Zach paced toward the window and back again. He rubbed the back of his neck absently. Finally, he nodded. "I'll do it." He sounded as if he'd agreed to be lined up against a wall and shot at.

"He shouldn't be much trouble. He's a

good kid, unlike some I know." She fixed a meaningful look on him.

Zach wanted to protest but held it in. No sense in letting on that he was terrified of taking a five-year-old out in public. He felt like a pansy enough without broad-casting his cowardice. "How long does it go on?"

"Starts at noon and runs till this evening, but you don't have to stay for the whole thing. Owen won't last that long."

"So what, maybe an hour?"

"Two or three, I'd say. Just tune in to the boy. He'll let you know when he's done."

Zach could tune in until he was old enough to retire, and he still didn't think he'd be able to read a kindergartner. He glanced at his watch. "Looks like we'd better go. Get it over with."

His grandma chuckled. "That's the spirit. Go have fun, Zachary. And if you don't mind, mail this pile of bills for me while you're out."

With a mock salute, he grabbed the stack of envelopes and left to search for Owen. He had a ton of work to catch up on—cor-respondence, bids, working up a plan for the zoning compromise. It was a nightmare to keep up on his job long distance. Yeah, Chuck had said to take some time off, but Zach didn't want Adam attempting something so important to the company. He'd just screw things up worse. Zach had no choice but to be here in Lone Oak, but he sure couldn't let his future go to pot by ignoring Moxley. He'd have to work half the night.

It took a full forty minutes to find Owen, wash his face, put some presentable clothes on the kid, herd him to the toilet, get shoes on him and head out the door. Forty minutes. He could've cleared his overflowing e-mail inbox in that time.

He took a slow breath and reminded himself it wasn't Owen's fault they were in this situation. All the boy did was have the bad luck of being born a Rundle.

"Let's go, O. See what this sock hop's all about."

"It's not a sock hop, it's a *carnival*." The child launched into explaining to Zach everything he thought they'd see there.

Outside, Zach opened the passenger

door to his truck and waited for Owen to hop in. The boy froze.

"Come on, don't you want to get to the carnival?"

Owen nodded fervently.

"Then what's wrong, buddy?"

"I need my booster."

"Your what?"

Owen headed for the garage while Zach tried to figure out what a booster was. Rocket engine? He followed the boy through the side door just in time to see him open the backseat of his grandma's old Buick.

"O, what are you doing? We're taking the truck. A much cooler ride than that old tank."

He finally saw what Owen tugged at— some kind of car seat. Ah, a booster seat. Of course.

Zach had been ready to drive down the road illegally, with Owen in nothing but a seat belt that probably wouldn't fit, now that he thought about it. Nice one. Good thing the kid was old enough to talk and smart enough to get what he needed.

He took the seat from the boy and

carried it to his truck. He squeezed it into the backseat and stared at it, wondering how to hook the thing up. He sighed. If they were lucky, they'd be home by bedtime.

"I'll do it." Owen squeezed under Zach's arms and wiggled into the backseat. He pushed the booster to the side, hopped up and pulled the shoulder belt across his scrawny body. "You're 'posed to buckle this in down there, then run it through this hole here."

Smart kid. Zach did as he was directed and they managed to pull out of the driveway in a mere five minutes.

At the carnival, they were bombarded by the screams and laughter of a thousand kids. Zach tried to ignore the headache that threatened him and told himself he wasn't out of his league. As they walked down the crowded hallway toward the gymnasium, Owen moved close to Zach and grasped his hand. The gesture startled Zach. He had this kid's trust, whether he deserved it or not.

The thought of what people would say when they saw *him* responsible for a young child made him sweat. Zach Rundle? Guiding a child? That was one for the books.

"Uncle Zach, look!" Owen squealed as they entered the gym, where most of the booths and attractions were set up.

He followed the boy's gaze to the giant inflatable slide looming over the crowd. He also spotted a dunking tank, a pie-throwing contest and a bunch of other activities. Zach hadn't been exposed to these kinds of community things until he was older. Then he'd stayed as far from them as possible.

Owen was bursting with excitement. Zach smiled in spite of himself. How could he not? This was what it should be like for a five-year-old boy.

They headed to the ticket booth and stocked up for the afternoon. Then he pulled Owen to the side and bent down so they could hear each other. "What do you want to do first, O?"

The child's eyes were bulging out of his face. It was obvious he couldn't wait to become part of the fray but instead of answering, he shrugged his shoulders.

"You don't know?"

Owen shook his head slowly and looked up at Zach fearfully. Zach would have to take the initiative here even though he was a novice—at carnivals *and* caretaking.

"How 'bout that big slide over there?" He gestured with his head.

Owen considered it but didn't reply.

"Looks pretty fun, doesn't it?"

A shy nod. Zach took that as a good sign and headed for the end of the slide line that snaked around two other attractions. As they waited, lots of kids about Owen's age wandered by, but Owen gave no sign of being friends with any of them. Sad. But not surprising. Rundles had trouble making friends.

When they got close to the front of the line, Zach said, "Looks like you have to take your shoes off." He bent down to help him, but Owen didn't move. "What's wrong, big guy?"

"You go, too."

"Me?"

Owen nodded.

"Go down the slide?"

"Yeah. Please, Uncle Zach?"

Zach stood and checked it out. He saw a mom come down it with a young child in her arms. Then a dad. Damn. He was hoping it wouldn't hold his weight. He'd feel like an idiot. "I don't know. Why don't you try it by yourself?"

Owen shook his head.

Time for Zach to suck it up.

"Okay, buddy. As long as you don't think I'm too big."

Owen giggled. "You're not too big! There's other daddies on it even."

Zach ignored the *other daddies* comment and bent to untie the work boots he always wore.

When it was their turn, Zach shelled out enough tickets for both of them and led Owen toward the inflatable stairs. They teetered like a couple of drunks on the unstable surface, which set Owen off in a fit of giggles. Zach boosted the boy's rear end when he needed it until they were at the top. As they prepared to launch, with Owen between Zach's legs, Zach glanced down at the crowd at the bottom.

Wouldn't you know it—there she was. The nosy sometimes-next-door neighbor easily stood out from the crowd with her huge smile and long hair pulled back into a ponytail. She wore a shirt unbuttoned halfway down with a tank underneath, drawing Zach's eyes to her breasts even from way up here. She waved across the way to someone just before she glanced up and saw Zach. Her smile faded.

"Let's go, Zach!"

They inched forward and plunged down the slide, Owen shrieking the whole way. Zach couldn't help but laugh right along with him. Forget the people watching. Especially her.

"Again! Again!" Owen hollered as he skittered out of the enclosed inflatable area.

Zach searched for Lindsey in the crowd, but he didn't see her. Just as well.

An hour later, after they'd exhausted their ticket supply, Zach and Owen made their way down the locker-lined hallway toward Food Alley. Zach caught the aroma of greasy fair foods—corn dogs, funnel cakes, bratwursts.

"What do you want, O?"

Owen stared at all the different booths, then shrugged.

Following his gut, Zach headed to a booth on their right. "Two turkey legs, please."

"We're eating legs?"

"Turkey. Haven't you had a turkey leg before?"

Owen shook his head.

"What about a chicken leg? A drumstick?"

"I guess so."

"This is just like a drumstick," Zach said after paying and taking the two big dripping legs from the cashier. "Except bigger."

They followed hand-painted signs to one of the classrooms designated a "picnic area." Several mismatched picnic tables covered in bright red checkerboard tablecloths and a barbeque grill for props were scattered around the room, the usual desks and chairs stacked along the far wall.

Lindsey sensed the moment Zach and his charge entered the room. She stood at the back, next to the sink, where she'd been washing off messy faces and hands before they returned to the gym.

She'd been shocked to see Zach here at

first. But it made sense that he'd brought Owen, who was the perfect age for the attractions. What had Mrs. Rundle had to do to convince Zach to chaperone? He couldn't be here by choice.

The tables some kids and their parents had just vacated needed a good cleaning—like maybe a power hose—so Lindsey grabbed a wet towel and headed over. When she got to the table next to Zach and Owen's, she couldn't help hearing their conversation.

"The main thing," Zach was saying, "is that you hold on to both sides. Especially the skinny part. It's like a handle." He showed Owen where to grasp the turkey leg. Owen was taking it in as if this were the most important lesson in the world.

Lindsey smiled. Owen was so trusting and happy, despite losing his mom and now his dad, too. He had a tenuous grip on the drumstick and sank his teeth into the meat. He giggled as grease dripped down his chin, and Zach reached across the table to wipe it up. Just as Zach finished, Owen spotted Lindsey and waved with his free hand. She waved back.

"Hi, Owen. Zach."

"Wanna sit with us?" Owen asked.

She glanced around. There were only three others in the room. No one needed her right now. And no one here would run to her dad.

"Come on, sit," Zach said.

There was no reason not to. She straddled the bench so she faced Owen, leaning on the table with one elbow.

"Didn't expect to see you here," Zach said between bites.

"My sister talked me into volunteering." She turned back to Owen. "How's the turkey leg?"

"Yummy! Uncle Zach's teaching me how to hold it."

"That's pretty nice of him. Might have to get one myself before long."

"Do you need Uncle Zach to teach you, too?"

"Nope. I'm an expert turkey leg eater." She forced her thoughts away from other things Zach could have taught her.

Zach raised a skeptical eyebrow at her, which she tried to ignore. She quizzed Owen about what games he'd played so far.

"My very favorite was the tank where you throw the ball at the circle and if you hit it, the person on the seat falls in the water."

"Ah, the dunk tank. Did you hit the circle?"

Owen shook his head. His eyes widened with excitement. "But Uncle Zach did. He got the principal wet. Everybody cheered."

Lindsey met Zach's eyes. "The principal, huh? Don't you know you're supposed to miss on purpose?"

"Had to come through for the kid."

Owen set down his half-eaten turkey leg and pushed it away. "All done?" she asked him.

He nodded and wiped his hands on his jeans. Lindsey gently took them and cleaned them with a napkin.

"If you take your garbage over there to that big trash can, I'll meet you at the sink in back to help you wash your hands and face."

"Not so fast," Zach said as he grabbed what remained of the leg. "I'll take care of this."

"You're so good with him," she said when Owen was out of earshot.

"Cut the crap, Salinger. My grandma and brother can take care of him fine."

"I was just making conversation."

He didn't answer, just pretended to be completely absorbed by the art of eating turkey.

"So Josh is home then?"

He glared. "Not yet."

"Then you're getting lots of practice with Owen." She grinned, knowing full well she was ticking him off.

He put down the turkey bone, mostly bare now, and wiped his chin with a napkin. Then he leveled his gaze at her. "There's no way I'm adopting him, so drop it."

She saw Owen waiting at the sink and stood. "I won't say another word. Today."

Zach shook his head. He was starting to believe she really did care about Owen. For some reason, that almost made Zach like her in spite of her incessant interfering.

Oh, who was he kidding? He'd always liked her. Too much. Especially when she wore low-cut tank tops that made him long for a closer look.

He sat where he was, waiting for Owen to return, when a short, older woman approached Lindsey.

"Hello, Lindsey," she said in a loud voice that seemed to fit her.

Owen headed back to Zach.

"Mrs. Seamore, hi... Grandma duty today, huh?" Lindsey looked toward the other end of the room, where two children sat across from each other eating watermelon.

"I'm giving Brynn a break. Who could pass up taking those two to a carnival?"

"They're cute. First and third grade?"

She nodded. Then the woman's voice got quieter, which, unfortunately, was still loud enough for Zach to hear. "I have to ask. What are you doing with Zach Rundle?"

She said *Rundle* the way she might say *prairie rattlesnake*. Zach didn't want to hear her, didn't want Owen to hear her, but he couldn't drag himself away.

"I..." Lindsey cleared her throat, looking caught off guard. "Owen—the little boy. I'm trying to make him feel comfortable. He's been through an awful lot."

"So I've heard." Mrs. Seamore's tone conveyed no warmth. "I don't think it's proper after what Josh did to your family."

"Come on, O, we're outta here." Zach pulled the child with him, wishing he'd left about five minutes sooner, knowing the boy had heard every word.

"What did my daddy do?" he asked as they left the classroom.

Zach wasn't going there today. "Nothing you need to worry about, kiddo. I promise it has nothing to do with you. I'll buy you six more tickets. What do you want to do?"

Lindsey glanced toward the door just as Zach led Owen out. They had to have heard Mrs. Seamore. She'd been one of her mom's best friends—they'd grown up together in Layton and had both ended up settling in Lone Oak. Lindsey knew she meant well, but why couldn't she just keep her mouth shut? She forced a smile and said, "Nice to see you again, Mrs. Seamore." As she moved away, she prayed the woman wouldn't get it in her head to call Lindsey's dad with the latest on his disrespectful daughter.

The Rundles' reputation had been shoddy for years, even before the accident. Josh and Zach had grown up with few if any friends and a laundry list of enemies. From the time they'd moved in with their grandma when their mom had reportedly deserted them, people had talked. Misfits from day one.

It appeared that Owen would be subjected to the same treatment as long as he stayed in this town.

For his sake, Lindsey wished there was an easy solution to the matter of his custody and care. Yeah, it'd be perfect if Josh surfaced and cleaned up his act in order to take over his role as father. But she seriously doubted that would happen anytime before Owen grew up and had kids of his own.

The more realistic solution was for Zach to step in and adopt him. Seeing him with his nephew today, she knew Zach could do it.

Growing up next door, Lindsey had had

glimpses beyond the bad-boy facade. At least with Zach. She'd known long before the accident he wasn't as bad as everyone wanted to believe. Wasn't even as bad as *he* wanted everyone to believe.

He used to put on an act anytime he was in public—at school when he'd bothered to show up, at the convenience store where he'd bought cigarettes. He'd played up the anti-authority rebel flawlessly. Lindsey imagined that was part of who he was. But she'd been exposed to a different side of him.

Zach cared more than anyone else would believe. He'd shown it earlier today in his own unsure-with-kids way. And he'd shown it years ago when Lindsey was maybe twelve years old and he'd saved her hide.

She'd been babysitting Katie, who was eight at the time, while her parents had taken Savannah somewhere—she didn't remember where. Katie had been overtired and wound up the whole day. A shipping box full of foam peanuts had been at the heart of the battle between Lindsey and her monster sister. After cleaning the pieces up countless times, Lindsey had forbidden Katie to play with them again, and when she'd done it anyway, Lindsey took the box out to the trash can in the garage. Katie had locked the back porch door, leaving Lindsey out in twenty-degree weather. If her parents had found out she'd been careless enough to leave Katie alone in the house, even for two minutes…. Never mind that Katie was the one being the brat.

Lindsey had tried everything to get inside and had been reduced to yelling threats from outside. At the height of her frustration, Zach had appeared out of the shadows.

"You trying to wake up the whole neighborhood?" he'd asked as he'd strutted across her yard, hands shoved into his pockets.

Not only had she had no control over her tantrum-throwing sister but he'd walked up on her when she'd been in the middle of her own tirade.

"My bratty sister locked me out," she'd explained. "If my parents get home and I'm out here, I'm in big trouble."

Instead of laughing at her or just

walking off as she'd expected, he'd come closer. "You need to get in the house?"

"My parents are supposed to get home any minute."

He'd leaned against the outside wall of the porch, looking casual, in control, so much older. Something about fourteen had seemed so grown up, and the way he'd looked down at her had made her nervous.

"We could do this the easy way or we could do it the fun way." His voice had sounded like an older boy's, low, smooth.

He'd glanced around the darkening backyard and up at the ancient tree that sheltered the part of the yard closest to the house.

"Wait here," he'd said as he jogged off to his grandma's garage. Two minutes later, he'd returned with a rope. He'd tossed it over a sturdy-looking branch, then had held on to both ends and lifted his legs off the ground to make sure it supported his weight. "I'll go first," he'd said. "Watch what I do, then follow me up."

Maybe she should've chosen the easy way.

Before she could answer, he had hoisted

himself up the trunk, using the rope for his hands and the trunk for his feet.

"Your turn." He'd kept his voice quiet, which she'd appreciated.

Taking a deep breath, she'd grabbed the rope ends he'd sent down for her. She hadn't wanted him to see her as a little kid who was afraid to join the adventure he'd started to save her.

To her surprise, he'd encouraged her in a soothing voice from above. Finally, she'd reached the lowest branch, the one Zach straddled. He'd pulled her up next to him.

"Not bad, for a girl."

She'd thought she saw a smile, but the last ounce of light had vanished from the sky. Lindsey remembered savoring the euphoria of being all the way up there, alone, with Zach.

"The branch that juts out to the porch roof by your window is right above us," he'd said. "Let's go."

When she'd lowered herself to the top of the porch, he'd steadied her briefly, his hands on her waist.

The window had been tougher to raise than either of them had expected. Finally, they'd managed to lift it enough for her to crawl through, just as headlights had lit up the garage door.

"My parents are home!" Her heart had raced in a panic.

The corners of his mouth had turned up as if this new development made it all the more fun. He'd met her eyes with his beautiful brown ones. "They won't know I'm here. Just go down and scare your bratty sister."

She'd scrambled in the window and had briefly leaned back through it to thank him, then had slammed it shut and rushed downstairs.

Later, when Lindsey had run back up to her room, Zach had been gone. She'd searched the tree branches and the yard below and had seen no trace of him. Even the rope had disappeared.

She'd had a crush on him ever since, if she was honest.

Lindsey felt certain he could learn to be a parent to Owen now. If only he'd step out from behind his blind insistence that his grandma and brother were fine.

CHAPTER NINE

THE TOWN OF ELLINGTON didn't have a lot going for it. The buildings on the main drag were in need of repair and some general care. Lone Oak had never thrilled Zach, but compared to this burg, it was like living in luxury.

It was the kind of place Josh would be drawn to, which was why Zach had cruised up and down the streets in search of his brother's old blue rust-bucket for hours the other day. Today he headed for the Rat's Nest first, hoping the guy who'd seen Josh before had more news for him.

He turned into the alley that ran behind the bar, then slowly pulled into one of the parking spots reserved for customers. It was more of an oversized pothole than a parking space. He got out and walked along the shabby brown brick exterior to the front entrance.

Inside, he stepped away from the door and let his eyes adjust to the darkness. There was nothing spectacular about this bar—it could be any one of a hundred small-town drinking dumps. Worn wood floor, dirty walls covered with beer and liquor signs, cheap tables and chairs.

Several tables were occupied, which said a lot about the town, considering it was just after four in the afternoon. Not lunch time, not happy hour, but plenty of drinkers. Who could blame them, living in a place like Ellington?

Zach glanced at each customer long enough to determine none were his brother. He hadn't figured, but he'd hoped anyway.

Then he turned toward the bar and did a double take. Josh was behind the bar serving up drinks. Or actually wiping the bar dry right now. Josh's eyes were on Zach instead of the towel.

Zach sauntered up to the bar and leaned on it. "What are you doing back there?"

"Fetching drinks. Want one?"

Zach hesitated, then asked for a Coke. "Been looking for you."

"It's your lucky day. You found me." Josh filled a glass, then set it in front of Zach. "What do you want?"

Zach absently turned the glass in a circle on the counter, then slid onto a stool. He took a long drink before speaking. "Gram said you'd been working at Dow's for nearly a year."

"Yep." Josh wasn't really hostile, but he wasn't friendly, either. No surprise there after their last contact in Gram's backyard.

"Said you'd gotten a raise a couple months ago."

"You need a loan or something?"

Zach chuckled halfheartedly. "Did you leave because of the kid?"

Josh didn't answer, just watched Zach warily and glanced at the clock.

"Are you actually an employee here or what?" Zach asked.

"For the past two days. Temporary, while his day help is out recovering from surgery."

"What time are you done?"

"Five."

Zach nodded, encouraged that Josh was being civil. "Finding out I had a five-year-old boy would send me running, too."

"Like hell."

Zach looked up sharply. "What's that mean?"

"You're the one with his life together. You wouldn't run."

"I've run before."

"Guess that's true." Josh looked over his shoulder at the mirror behind the bar that Zach guessed was a one-way window. "What'd you come here for?"

"To find you."

"I know that. What d'you want?"

"I got the impression the other night that you care about your son."

"Yeah, I care about him. Why do you think I left?"

Zach felt an unfamiliar pang of sympathy. The two of them were about as dysfunctional as they came.

"Owen needs you."

"Nah. He needs Granny. She knows what she's doing."

"He needs a man. A dad. Someone to play catch and whatever else it is normal families do."

Josh laughed. "I'm no normal family. Come on, look at me. This ain't what Owen needs."

"You could do it, Josh."

Josh glanced toward the tap. Was he longing for a drink? Zach would put money on it.

One of the men in the corner booth hollered out for two more bottles. Josh grabbed the order from the cooler as the guy ambled to the bar and put down several ones. "Keep the change."

Josh shuffled through the bills and muttered that the extra fifty cents wouldn't change his life. He took his time putting the cash away and Zach figured he wanted to avoid him. Tough.

"Why not give it a go?" Zach said to his back.

"Tried it. Didn't work out."

"Two weeks isn't a fair trial. This is parenting, not riding a bike."

Josh sighed and leaned his elbows on the counter, rubbing his scruffy face with both hands. "Granny said I was stinking up the whole thing."

"Is that why you left?"

"She knows so much, she can take care of him."

"She was trying to help you."

The pensive look on Josh's face made Zach think maybe he was getting somewhere. "You could probably get your job back. That boy is aching for a dad."

Josh closed his eyes. His silence was a positive sign. If he had a complaint or an argument, he sure wouldn't hold it in.

"Gram will be there. A built-in babysitter…"

"I don't know. I don't want to mess him up."

Zach understood all too well. "I'll stick around for a couple of weeks, until you get your bearings. I'm no role model but we can figure it out. Gram and I talked. We both want to help you do this."

"How are you gonna help me?"

"I'll just be around. I found a group for single dads. They meet, shoot the breeze, talk about stuff. They're all going through the same thing as you."

Josh looked like he was honestly considering it.

"Think what it'd be like to know your son, to see him grow up. Just to be a part of his life, man."

Josh nodded with a look of fear on his face.

Fear was good. That meant he took the responsibility seriously, and that gave Zach hope.

"He's a great kid, Josh. He deserves to have a dad."

Josh looked at the clock again, and just as he did, a tall woman flew in from the back office. "I'm here. Sorry I'm late."

Josh didn't say a word. He went back to the office, then reappeared a minute later. Zach wondered if he was going to take off, but Josh took the stool next to him. "Let me have one drink while I think about it. Cool?"

Zach nodded and asked the woman for another Coke.

It was two bourbons and a couple of burgers later, but Zach finally got Josh to agree to come home.

Part one of the battle was over. Zach only hoped that was the hardest part.

LINDSEY PULLED INTO HER dad's driveway. She climbed out, then leaned back inside to yank her bag from the passenger side, where it was stuck on the lever underneath the seat. She straightened to find Owen standing inches away from her, making her drop her bag.

"Owen! What are you doing here, sweetie?" Trying to sound normal when her heart was in her throat was a challenge.

"Wanna play?"

She looked across the backyards, expecting to see either Zach or his grandma bearing down on them, but there was no one in sight. Had he snuck out again?

"Where's your uncle Zach?"

Owen shrugged. "He left."

"Back to Wichita?" She hated that she felt a smidge of disappointment.

"I dunno where he went."

"Does your grandma know you're outside?"

"I dunno." Confusion crossed his face.

"Is something wrong, Owen?"

He hesitated, then shook his head.

"Well." What to do. Her dad would be

lurking inside, hungry for dinner. But Lindsey was curious about Mrs. Rundle. Maybe it was nothing. But maybe it wasn't…once again.

She set her purse and shoulder bag full of work down on the driveway next to the porch. "How about if we play follow the leader for a couple minutes before I take you home?"

"Okay! I'm the leader."

She smiled and groaned at the same time as Owen headed off into the yard at a full gallop. Heels in marshy grass. Bad combination. She followed him, trying to put all her weight on her toes.

Owen ran circles around her dad's backyard, arms out like an airplane with audio to match. Lindsey followed suit, trying not to laugh.

She intended to give him a minute or so to be the leader, then when her turn came, she'd lead him toward his own back door. A minute turned out to be too long, though.

Just as they were marching past the back porch, Lindsey caught a glimpse of a face in the kitchen window. Her dad.

Damn.

Her instinct was to run inside and explain why she was with Owen, but in truth it would make no difference. Her dad would nod and try to act like it was okay, but the look on his face would give away his sadness, anger, disappointment, whatever it was churning inside him at the moment.

She waved but got no response.

"Okay, Owen, time to get you home."

Giggling, thankfully unaware of her dad's disapproval, Owen trotted ahead of her to his back door.

No one answered when they knocked. Lindsey waited and then pounded on the door again.

"Your grandma was home when you left?"

Owen nodded. Lindsey glanced at the open garage. Her Buick was parked inside.

Tentatively, Lindsey opened the door. "Hello?"

No one answered, so she took Owen's hand and crept inside. Walking into the house uninvited was disquieting, to say the least. So was the vague fear of what she might find.

They searched the rooms on the main level but didn't find Mrs. Rundle. Before heading up the stairs, Lindsey called again. No one answered, but she thought she heard a noise.

Her heart pounded as they climbed. What if she found her dead or something? Unconscious?

"Can you show me which room is your grandma's?" she asked Owen.

Still holding her hand and looking more frightened by the second, he led her to the room at the far end of the hallway. The door was wide open and she knew before she could see that someone was in there.

"Mrs. Rundle?" she said as she peeked in.

"I can't find the darn things anywhere."

Well, at least she wasn't dead.

She was bent over, rummaging through her closet, which was piled about two feet high with…junk. Shoes, boxes, plastic bags. It was no wonder something was lost.

Owen dropped Lindsey's hand and rushed forward. "Hi, Grandma!"

The older woman looked at him distractedly. "I know I had them earlier."

"What are you looking for?" Lindsey asked.

"House shoes." She reached to the far corner of the closet, muttering something Lindsey couldn't understand. She seemed way too distressed about her slippers.

"Have you looked everywhere else?"

"I keep my house shoes in my closet." She said this in a tone that warned Lindsey not to argue.

Just then, Lindsey heard a door slam downstairs. She hoped it was Zach, for multiple reasons.

Mrs. Rundle was becoming more frustrated.

"Why don't you sit down for a minute?" Lindsey said. When the woman ignored her, she gently took her by the elbow. "It's okay. We'll find them."

"What's going on? Lindsey? What are you doing here?" Zach stood at the doorway. "Gram? You okay?"

His grandma didn't look at him.

"She says she can't find her slippers," Lindsey said, as if that could explain why his grandma was so flustered and upset.

Zach stepped into the room. "Slippers? Those?" He nodded toward the head of Mrs. Rundle's bed and Lindsey saw a pair of yellow slippers poking halfway out from under the bed skirt.

Owen jumped over and picked them up. "Here they are, Grandma." He handed them to her, clearly wanting to make her feel better.

Upon seeing the slippers, Mrs. Rundle took a deep breath, then hung her head. She looked close to tears. Zach glanced questioningly at Lindsey.

"Put these on, Gram. I'll see Lindsey out."

Resigned, his grandma slowly lowered herself to the edge of the bed and Owen climbed up next to her.

Zach and Lindsey left the room. At the top of the stairs, they stopped. "What the devil is going on?" he asked.

Lindsey explained how Owen had wandered over to her dad's house and what they'd found when she brought him back home. "She was like that when we found her."

Zach furrowed his brow. When Lindsey touched his forearm, he stiffened.

"She'll be okay," he said. "She's probably just tired. She insisted on cleaning the whole house today."

Lindsey suspected it was a lot more than tired. "Maybe you should go back to the doctor."

"We'll see what happens."

She could tell he didn't want to admit that was necessary, but she didn't have time to argue right now.

"I need to get home. My dad is likely beside himself."

"Because you're here?"

"You got it." She started down the stairs.

"Lindsey, wait. Josh is home."

She stopped cold.

She'd seen him at a distance from time to time over the years, but the thought of facing him chilled her blood.

Zach caught up to her. "I'll let you out the front door," he said simply.

When she didn't move, he touched her arm, urging her forward. Startled, she looked up at him. The empathy in his expression nearly undid her and for a weak moment she wanted to bury herself in his arms.

She could hear rustling from the other room—the click of a lamp switch, a glass clinking on a table, the buzz of the TV coming on. Everyday sounds. *His* life went on as usual while her mom would never take another drink, would never watch the TV again. Lindsey shuddered.

The door was directly in front of her. Lindsey descended the rest of the stairs and made a beeline out.

"Thanks for trying to calm Gram down," Zach said when she was on the outside step.

She didn't turn around, didn't take the time to answer. She just put as much distance as she could between herself and Josh Rundle.

ZACH TURNED AFTER SEEING Lindsey out to find Owen hovering at the top of the stairs.

"I miss Lindsey," the boy said.

"She just left, O. You can't miss her yet."

Owen frowned.

"Go get Gram and come downstairs. There's someone here to see you."

Owen looked confused. "Lindsey?"

"She just went out the door." Zach laughed. So his nephew was a sucker for a pretty face.

Actually, he knew it went beyond that. Lindsey was the only one among them who had a special touch with kids. He could hardly blame Owen for gravitating to her, though they'd have to talk about impromptu visits next door. From what Zach knew of old man Salinger, Owen needed to learn to stay away. Zach could take the negative opinions, the comments, the looks, but he didn't want that for Owen.

Owen and Gram made their way down.

"Who's here?" Owen said excitedly.

Gram looked hopeful but cautious. Zach motioned them into the living room, where Josh lounged on Gram's favorite chair.

"Joshua." Gram wasn't an emotional woman, but her tone spoke a world of feeling. Relief. Affection.

"Hi, Granny."

He rose and she wrapped her skinny arms around him, tiredly looking him over from head to toe. "I'm glad you're back."

Josh made no bones about being happy to be home, but he smiled as Gram took her seat back.

Zach waited for Owen to react to his dad. A big welcoming hug would go a long way right now. But none came. The kid stared at the TV, and he sat on the farthest end of the couch.

"Owen. Your daddy's home."

Owen looked at Josh, gave a distracted half smile. "Hi." Then went back to the reality show.

Zach glanced at Josh and knew his son's cool reception was getting to him. "Go sit next to him."

Josh glared at Zach but sauntered across the living room. He sat on the couch close to Owen. Zach turned off the TV. After a long silence, Josh said, "How you been, Owen?"

"Fine."

Zach paced into the kitchen. He needed this to go a hell of a lot better if it was going to work.

His grandma came in then. "Where'd you find him?"

"That bar I told you about. Took a lot of talking to get him home, and now Owen's treating him like a stranger."

"They *are* strangers. That boy knows you better than he knows his father."

"They were together for two weeks, weren't they?"

"Manner of speaking. Joshua wasn't around much."

No wonder Owen didn't care more. But that was the past, and Josh needed to work on the future. For everyone's sake.

Zach went back into the living room to find Josh still next to Owen, both of them staring at the TV, which had been turned on again.

"What's that guy's name?" Josh asked Owen, pointing at the screen.

"Your breath smells stinky!"

Nice. Probably bourbon. Josh *had* to ease up on the booze.

"Owen, that's your favorite guy he's talking about, isn't it? What's his name?" Zach found it incredibly awkward to force Owen to acknowledge his father.

"It's Joe," Owen said.

Silence fell over them. Zach wandered over to the couch and sat down away from them. He had a ton of work to do, but he didn't want to leave these guys alone. He wasn't sure he trusted Josh not to take off again or Owen not to antagonize Josh.

Zach's head was reclined way back on the couch cushion, and he was just about to doze off when he felt Owen climb up next to him. What the hell? He'd never cuddled up to him before. Now that Josh was home and Zach needed them to bond, here he came curling up next to *him*. He couldn't turn him away, though. He forced a smile and hoisted Owen up on his lap, hoping, for Josh's sake, Owen would get uncomfortable quickly.

Gram shuffled to her chair, and they all watched the rest of the show without speaking. When it ended, Gram took charge, as usual, the slipper scene seemingly forgotten.

"Time for bed, Owen. Go brush your teeth."

"Zach, will you read me a story tonight?"

Zach glanced at Josh, who was pretending not to listen.

"Why don't you let your daddy read to you? He hasn't seen you for a long time. I bet he's missed you like crazy."

Josh looked at Owen then, who was still on Zach's lap, and nodded. "Yep. Sure have." He attempted a smile.

Owen turned around to face Zach. "I want you to read, Zach. Please?"

Zach closed his eyes briefly. Any night but this one. Every night but tonight. "If you're sure your daddy can't do it."

"I want *you*."

"Get up there, then. I'll be up in a minute."

Owen climbed down from his lap and took off.

"This was a mistake," Josh said.

"Give him a break, man. He hasn't seen you for weeks. He just needs time to get used to you."

Josh hopped up and went to the kitchen. Gram exchanged a worried look with Zach, and then they heard Josh open a beer can.

"He's gotta stop drinking," Gram said.

Zach nodded. "Let's just get through day one first."

His grandma nodded wearily. "You take care of Owen. I'm going to talk to Joshua then hit the hay. Thanks for bringing him home, Zachary."

Zach wasn't altogether convinced now that it was a good thing.

WHEN ZACH CAME BACK downstairs after reading to Owen, he heard someone in the kitchen, putting dishes away.

"Where's Josh?" he asked Gram.

She didn't look at him. "He left. Said he'll be back later."

"He *is* coming back?"

"Said he was. Who knows, with that boy."

"This isn't going well."

"No. Maybe we should talk to Owen, get him to open up a bit more."

"Can't force that. Kids are honest, Gram. He doesn't like Josh. Doesn't trust him." Zach leaned against the counter and pounded his fist against the drawer behind him. "He damn well better not disappear."

CHAPTER TEN

LINDSEY BENT OVER FOR the zillionth time and scooped the load of snow that she swore would be the one to break her back. Three inches had fallen overnight, and while that wasn't a huge amount, it was the heavy, wet, muscle-taxing kind of snow. Her dad owned a snowblower, but she'd had some noble idea about getting some exercise.

She'd made it to his house at a decent hour tonight. It'd been a particularly depressing day, one filled with the frustrating bureaucracy that made her feel helpless. She hadn't hesitated to walk out the door at five o'clock for once. Since soup was in the slow-cooker, there was time to clear the driveway before all the light disappeared.

The blessedly narrow driveway was

almost halfway cleared when a horrible crash echoed through the air. Her dad's house stood between her and the Rundles', but she was positive the noise came from their direction. Without thought, she took off in a combination slide-run across the shoveled part of the driveway and through the adjoining back-yards.

Once she cleared Zach's shop, she stopped abruptly at the sight before her. Mrs. Rundle's car, the yacht-sized gas guzzler that'd seen better days, stuck out of the back of the garage at an odd angle.

Fear paralyzed her for what seemed like minutes but was probably just a few seconds. Accidents did that to her, any-more.

Lindsey snapped from her stupor and propelled herself through the snow. From the garage door, she saw Owen's head just barely visible above the top of the backseat. And then she heard his cries.

She rushed to the back door on the driver's side and whipped it open. Owen's mouth gaped in terror, but he appeared to be physically unharmed. Lindsey reached across him to release the seat belt and picked him up.

"I'm scared," he said and his lower lip trembled.

Only then did she turn her attention to the woman collapsed over the steering wheel.

She hurriedly set Owen down. "Stay right there, sweetie." Realizing her own panic was scaring him more, she placed a kiss on his forehead. "It's okay, Owen. You're okay. I'm going to help your great-grandma now."

She shut the back door with her hip, but before she could get to the front one, Zach shoved past her from out of nowhere.

"Gram!"

The woman sat up and looked at him, thank goodness. With tears in her eyes, she shook her head. "I screwed up." Her voice was high-pitched and shaky. "I put it in Drive."

"Did you hit your head, Grandma?" Zach asked.

She paused, confused. "No. Don't think I did. My body's okay."

"I'm calling an ambulance."

"Don't you dare, Zachary. Help me get out of here."

"What's wrong with Grandma?" Owen asked.

Leaning down and picking him up again, Lindsey answered. "She's sad. But she'll be okay."

Zach had a panicked look in his eyes and he clenched his hands in and out of fists. "Should I move her?"

"I think it's fine. She said she's okay, Zach."

"Shit," he said as he glanced at the car where it jutted through the garage. "Come on, Gram. Let's get you inside."

"Is your brother home?" Lindsey asked quietly.

Zach shook his head, clearly annoyed.

She took Owen out of the way, toward the house.

"Why is Grandma sad?" Owen asked.

Lindsey ignored the odd feeling of walking through the back door again and tried to make herself at home. "She's sad because her car is messed up. And the garage." *And she might be forced to face the possibility that something is very wrong with her.* She searched for a means of distracting Owen. "How about if we color her a picture to make her feel better?"

Owen had a different idea, though. He dragged one of the kitchen chairs to the window, climbed up on it, and gazed out toward the garage.

"How come Grandma broke her car?"

"It was an accident, sweetie. She didn't mean to. Instead of making the car go backward, she made it go forward."

Owen turned to look at her, trying to understand. She guided him to sit on the chair and slid it back to the table with him on it.

"We'll need a tow truck," he declared.

Lindsey smiled in spite of the circumstances. Sneaking a peek outside, she nodded. "We might. The important thing is that you and your grandma weren't hurt." At least not badly. Would Mrs. Rundle be okay?

Owen turned back to the window, as if drawn by some magnetic force.

"Are you hungry?"

He shook his head and didn't budge.

Over his shoulder, Lindsey saw Zach and Mrs. Rundle emerge from the garage. Zach's arm was hooked with his grandma's and they moved at a turtle's pace. Mrs. Rundle looked terrible, and Zach looked strung out himself.

Lindsey still had half her dad's driveway to shovel, but it would have to wait. He wasn't allowed to drive yet, anyway, and Mrs. Hale was still out of town. "I have an idea," she said to Owen. "Let's go sledding." She had no clue what she'd tell her dad.

Her suggestion got Owen's interest.

"Yeah!" He climbed down from the chair and zipped across the kitchen, the accident forgotten for the time being. "I got snow pants and boots!"

"Let's ask your Uncle Zach first to make sure it's okay."

When Zach and Mrs. Rundle came in, Owen nearly pounced on them. "Uncle Zach, can I go sledding with Lindsey?"

Zach shot a confused look toward her.

"There's a hill behind the house Brooke and I live in. I thought maybe it'd be good for us to get out of your way…?"

He nodded distractedly. "Sure. Yeah, go for it."

"Can I do anything to help before we go?" Lindsey asked.

"I don't know. I'm not sure what to do. She doesn't want a doctor."

Lindsey touched his hand and gently took his place supporting the older woman.

"Mrs. Rundle, why don't we get you to a comfortable chair in the living room?"

Mrs. Rundle made eye contact with her, and Lindsey read a mix of emotions there. Fear seemed the most obvious.

The years of bad blood slipped away, and Lindsey had the urge to comfort the woman. She could only imagine what it must feel like to be in her shoes, unable to trust herself to even drive the car.

"Let's go," Lindsey said when the woman didn't move. She patted Mrs. Rundle's elbow and urged her forward. She didn't fuss when Lindsey kept a hold on her as she lowered herself into the chair.

"Thank you." Mrs. Rundle sounded like she'd just run a marathon.

"Can I get you something warm to drink? Coffee or cocoa?"

"I'd take a cup of coffee. Black and strong."

"Zach?"

He stood in the doorway between the kitchen and living room. "Sure. Same."

She'd meant for him to make the coffee, but he didn't seem to be functioning well. His vulnerability surprised her, would've made her smile in a different, happier situation. "Take a load off," she told him. When she walked past him, she couldn't resist touching his arm. Their eyes met. Afraid of the warmth that seemed to pass between them, Lindsey tried to drop her hand, but Zach grasped her fingers. Long enough to squeeze them gently.

She didn't want to acknowledge the way the gesture warmed her, so she switched back to business mode and went about prepping the coffeemaker.

Owen came waddling into the kitchen just as the soothing drip of the coffee started a few minutes later. He had snow pants around his ankles but apparently couldn't get them up over his jeans by himself. He'd also thrown on a Spider-Man stocking cap and dragged his coat and boots behind him. Lindsey knelt to help him bundle up the rest of the way, and by the time they finished, the coffee was almost brewed.

"I have to pee," Owen said, as Lindsey got two mugs out of the cabinet.

She laughed and knelt to undo everything they'd just done up. At this rate, she'd be exhausted before they ever got to the hill. Kids took a lot of energy. She'd always been aware of that, but the past half hour with Owen was hammering it home. How could an eighty-year-old woman—or an alcoholic man, for that matter—expect to be both mother and father to Owen?

After today, Zach would have to seriously consider an alternative. She couldn't help but sympathize with him. It was a major decision, even though the obvious answer stared him in the face. Adopting Owen would change Zach's life forever, but there was no doubt in Lindsey's mind that's what had to happen.

ZACH HAD FINALLY convinced his grandma to lie down for a while, and she'd ended up falling asleep in minutes. She needed rest badly—the wreck had taken a lot out of her.

It figured Josh wasn't home when it happened. Not that he could've or would've done much, but Zach was out of his league. He'd lost it when he'd seen Gram slumped over the wheel. All kinds of crazy thoughts had screamed through his head. She was dead. She was paralyzed. She was bleeding all over the place. Thankfully she was relatively fine. He had no idea why he'd been unable to react calmly. Normally he was cool and collected in a crisis, but today he'd been useless.

Zach turned his truck onto Lindsey's street and searched for numbers on the houses. He'd gotten the address from the phone book, and though he wasn't sure which exact house she lived in, there wasn't a part of town he wasn't familiar with.

As soon as Gram had slipped into a deep sleep, he'd decided to go after Owen.

When Lindsey had carted him off, Zach hadn't thought twice about it. Now that things had calmed down, he felt like a clod for saddling her with a child she shouldn't have to take care of. No matter how much it burned him up that Josh wasn't taking responsibility, he wasn't going to let outsiders suffer for it. Owen was his family's responsibility and no one else's, and Zach intended to keep it that way.

He didn't relish talking to her, seeing that knowing I-told-you-so look. Hitting Drive instead of Reverse was a mistake anyone could make. It didn't mean Gram was losing her mind.

He pulled up to the end of the block, struggling to see the house numbers in the darkness. Hers was the last one before the street came to a dead end. It was an old house, as most in Lone Oak were, with a porch that ran along the front. Clean white paint disguised the need for new clapboard siding, and an old-fashioned lantern brightened the path to the porch.

As he climbed the uneven steps, the porch seemed lived-in, comfortable, in spite of the snow and cold. A wooden rocker was angled next to the door, and a pine swing hung at one end. Several pots were scattered about, and Zach had no doubt they'd be full of bright flowers in the spring.

A cutesy wreath of white branches on the front door proclaimed a welcome, but before he could knock, he recognized Owen's and Lindsey's shrieks—happy ones—coming from the backyard. He descended the stairs and trudged through the snow to the back of the house.

The first thing he saw was hair. Lots of it. Brown waves, plenty of tangles. It flew out behind the duo, who were halfway down the short but steep hill. They'd both piled onto a saucer sled, with Lindsey cross-legged and Owen on her lap. Both of them held on for dear life, the woman to the sled and the boy to the woman. At the bottom of the slope, they collapsed in a tangle of arms, legs and giggles. Double spotlights attached to the house lit the yard, illuminating the scene, making the snow sparkle.

Lindsey's sense of fun was foreign to him. Refreshing. She didn't merely succumb to pressure to participate in the crazier aspects of life—like playing with a child. She jumped in with both feet and a contagious grin on her face. Watching her, you'd think sliding down a bank of snow in twenty-degree weather was her favorite thing in the world.

Zach stood near the house, hands in pockets, watching as the two tromped up the hill. Lindsey held Owen's hand and he jabbered the whole way.

They didn't notice Zach until they were a few feet from him. The smile faded from Lindsey's face and she pulled Owen close.

"Is something wrong?"

"No, no. Gram's sleeping." He shifted his weight, feeling out of place for intruding on their fun. Clearly, he was the odd man out. "I thought I'd pick up Owen to save you the trip," he said, unwilling to reveal that he felt like he'd slipped up by letting Owen go out with her.

She visibly relaxed, and as she smiled and brushed a stray hair off her face, his attention was drawn to that damn dimple. She noticed him staring. She fidgeted and looked away, her confidence faltering.

That sudden insecurity took him by surprise.

She looked at Owen. "Your cheeks are getting red, kiddo. Probably a good time to call it quits and warm up."

"Are we going in your house to have hot chocolate?" Owen asked.

Tired of playing spectator, Zach jumped in. "We need to get home and make sure Grandma's still sleeping. We'll see if there's any cocoa there."

Owen looked to Lindsey, and Zach tried not to let it bother him. If he were in Owen's shoes, he'd like Lindsey a lot better, too. When she nodded, the boy sped ahead of them toward the front yard and Zach's truck.

"I'm going back to my dad's, you know. It wouldn't have been a problem for me to bring Owen home."

"I shouldn't have let him come over here in the first place."

Lindsey stopped. "I don't mind helping out with him. I'm not keeping a list and holding things against you, Zach."

"He's not your responsibility."

She began walking again, and he fell into step with her.

"You've got your hands full, between Owen and your grandmother. I'm not much help with her, but I can sled with the best of them."

Ah, his grandma. Here it came. The lecture on how she'd been right. He waited, irritated.

But she didn't say a word. He glanced at her.

"What?" she asked.

Zach shrugged. He wasn't going to bring it up if she wasn't.

"You want to talk about your grandma?"

It was eerie how she knew what was on his mind. "Not particularly. But I figured you'd be all over me about her."

They faced each other as they reached the back of his truck. Owen had climbed in and closed his door. She could see him—barely—working on buckling his seat belt.

"I didn't want to be right." Her voice was soft, gentle. He wanted to believe her.

How was it she continually had him off balance? He was used to being in charge, used to having control—over himself and others. Lindsey tended to surprise him. Pull the opposite of what he expected.

"Any idea what you're going to do next?"

Again, it was her tone. Not condescending. No hint of victory. Just... concern. Interest.

"I don't know." Three little words that seemed huge. "Take her back in, I guess. Might be time for a specialist."

Lindsey nodded. "A neurologist. I think there's one in Manhattan, but Topeka's your best bet."

"I might bring her to Wichita with me. Then I could take care of some business while I'm there."

"What about Owen?"

"I still don't know, Lindsey."

"I meant while you do business in Wichita. You wouldn't leave him with Josh, would you?"

He shared her irritation with his brother. Her emotions went far beyond irritation, but he agreed—right now, he couldn't leave Owen with Josh. Not if he couldn't trust Josh to be sober.

Zach shook his head and looked away.

"The deal with Josh—it's not going as well as I'd hoped." He really hated owning up to that. He still thought they could turn things around, but it wouldn't happen until he got Josh to stop drinking. To do that, Josh had to be home long enough for them to talk.

"He doesn't want to be there?"

"That's the thing. I think he does. But he hasn't stayed home for more than a couple hours at a time. He doesn't know what to do with Owen." Which was all too familiar to Zach. "Anyway, if I have to, I can take O with me to Wichita. My boss's wife would love to watch him."

She was thoughtful, and thankfully silent, but he knew that wasn't the end of it. He focused on the faint, lone freckle near her left cheekbone and found himself wanting to run his finger over it. He hadn't noticed it before. Did makeup cover more freckles or was it the only one?

"We've talked about a solution before, you know." Lindsey looked at the ground when she said it, knowing he'd protest.

"Lindsey. You can't think my adopting him would be best for Owen."

"Why not?"

"I'm not cut out—" He stopped talking when she pressed her mittened hand to his chest.

"You don't have to commit to it tonight," she said quietly. "Owen loves you. He trusts you, Zach. He'd rather be with you than anyone."

Zach looked off to the side, down the street, and Lindsey stepped to the edge of the curb, until she was inches away from him and nearly eye level. She studied his profile—his jaw wasn't locked as it frequently was when they argued. His lips were parted slightly, and his expression was one of trepidation.

He didn't acknowledge that she'd moved closer, so Lindsey shoved her mittens in her pocket and brushed his cheek lightly with her bare fingers. He turned his face toward her, finally met her gaze. Her fingers found his and grasped them, just the tips.

She didn't know if she leaned closer for her sake or for his. Wasn't aware of making a conscious decision. All she knew was that he was way too down on himself, and she didn't want him to be.

The idea of kissing him was never really

a coherent thought, but the closer they got, the more impossible it was not to. When her lips were a breath from his, she heard a faint warning in the back of her mind, but the pull of the man in front of her was far stronger.

His mouth was warm and moist, in spite of the cold and wind. She started to pull away to gauge his reaction, but she wanted another taste. A longer one. Their lips met again, and his hand moved to her hip, his fingers applying enough pressure to keep her close. Their other hands were still entwined, and he tightened his grip. She leaned into him, feeling heat where their bodies met, from chest to thighs, despite their winter coats.

She wrapped her arms around him, needing him nearer. The world around them fell out of focus and Lindsey's entire being centered on the sensations this man was causing. Light-headedness. Heat. Aching need.

He pulled her body into his, letting her feel his desire. She ran her fingers through his hair, drawing him to her possessively.

Every nerve in her body was connected to him, longing for his touch.

Without warning, Zach broke the contact of their lips and drew his head back. Confused, Lindsey blinked up at him.

He wouldn't meet her eyes. He straightened, which forced Lindsey to take a step back away from the edge of the curb, away from the warmth of his body. Away from what she'd thought felt like magic.

"I need to get Owen home."

The cool air blew between them, and Lindsey took another step back. She'd been rejected by Zach before, and she had no earthly clue why she'd just given in to the desire to kiss him again.

"Yeah. So go." *Walk away. Leave me feeling like an idiot.*

He paused to brush her hair behind her ear. She could swear there was tenderness in the gesture, some kind of feeling for her behind it.

But then he stalked off, making his way to the driver's side of the truck. Before opening the door, he said, "Thanks, Salinger," then got in.

She was back to being Salinger.

As Zach started the engine, she made a point of waving to Owen. When he didn't wave back, she realized his head tipped at an angle that could only mean he'd fallen asleep. Bless his heart, she'd worn him out.

She didn't wave to Zach. She'd already given him too much tonight.

Zach revved it and turned around in her driveway. He flew out of there as fast as he could in spite of the snowy street. Without glancing sideways, he knew she hadn't moved, sensed she stood there and watched the truck until it disappeared around the corner.

Why had he let that kiss happen?

He scoffed. Obviously because he'd wanted it, every bit of it and more.

Zach flipped the radio on. As loud as he dared with a sleeping kid. He fought to listen to the lyrics, but his mind kept returning to that kiss.

Not even a deep kiss. He'd barely touched her for longer than a few seconds. Yet he could still feel his blood pounding. He could still discern the scent of her hair as it blew around his face.

He didn't like to feel. Didn't like to want so much. Rational thoughts were safer and far easier than these out-of-control emotions.

Lindsey could turn him into a mindless idiot with a single touch, and that was something he couldn't afford. There was too much at stake with her. She had the power to open up too much of him. There was no future for them, no point in him wanting anything from her. He knew damn well a woman like her couldn't love a man like him.

Once he could settle things down for his grandma, Josh and Owen, it was back to Wichita, back to his life. The one he had control over.

CHAPTER ELEVEN

LINDSEY TOOK TIME TO GO inside and change out of her damp clothes before returning to her dad's house. She didn't want to follow Zach directly. She didn't want to see him, didn't want to think about what had just happened. She'd beaten herself up enough already.

Twenty minutes later, she pulled up to the curb at her dad's. She hopped out without a glance next door. She was nervous enough about facing her dad, even though there was no way he could know she'd kissed Zach. Giving another moment's analysis to her spontaneous stupidity would make her nauseous.

Thank goodness for slow-cookers. Before she'd gone outside to shovel the driveway, she'd told her dad to eat when he was hungry, not to wait for her. So at least he wasn't sitting around waiting for dinner.

Instead, he sat at the kitchen table waiting for *her*.

She'd been hoping she could slip in unnoticed…that he'd fallen asleep or gotten caught up in a crossword puzzle or… something.

"Where have you been?" His voice was relatively quiet, so it was a safe guess he didn't know about the accident next door.

"There was a minor accident nearby. I went to help."

She didn't look directly at him, busied herself with spooning out a bowl of soup. *Please, let it drop.*

"Where was the accident?"

Lindsey's back was to him as she sawed off a thick slice of sunflower bread. "Next door. No one was hurt." She turned and brought the food to the table.

He held back a comment—she could actually see him consciously bite down on it.

Lindsey sat across from him and ate in silence.

It would kill him if he found out she'd kissed Zach.

She'd kissed *him,* for God's sake. She had every reason not to look at Zach, let alone touch him. If she was brutally honest, she'd loved it, too. She hadn't given her dad's feelings a thought until later.

Well, one thing was certain. She'd pushed Zach farther away by kissing him. She wouldn't have to worry about anything deeper developing between them. Maybe her dumb move was a good thing after all.

She absently stirred her soup.

"Have you heard from Mrs. Hale today?" Lindsey asked when she could no longer stand the quiet.

Her dad mumbled an affirmative.

"Is she coming home soon?"

"You tired of babysitting?"

"I'm not babysitting. I'm helping you out when you need it." Just liked she always had. She had no problem with it, and he never had, either. Until now.

"Hmph."

"You've been a grump since she left."

"You try sitting in the same house, day after day, while people screw up your newspaper. I'm going stir-crazy, Lindsey."

"You two have something going on I should know about, Dad?"

"Who two?"

"You and Mrs. Hale."

He wouldn't look her in the eye. "Nah, nothing going on. She's a good woman to put up with me."

"You can say that again." Lindsey took a bite of bread and watched him while she chewed. "You care about her."

"I just said—"

"I mean beyond that. More than a friend."

He seemed flustered, didn't say anything for a few seconds. "Just a friend," he finally muttered. "I'm going to read and hit the sack."

Which spoke volumes.

The idea would take some getting used to, but he deserved to find someone to make him happy. He'd spent so many years mourning his wife and devoting all his energy to his job.

Searing regret burned Lindsey's chest

when she thought about his pain—all because she'd begged her mom to go to a movie with her on the wrong night at the wrong time.

As her dad left the room, Lindsey closed her eyes and concentrated on blocking out her thoughts. Focused on anything but her mom's accident. She was skilled at it after so many years.

Lindsey poured the rest of her soup down the sink. Guilt had a way of killing the best of appetites.

ELSA SAT LISTLESSLY at the kitchen table, waiting for Zach and Owen to come home for lunch the next day. Joshua was holed up in his room. There seemed to be a wide rift between them since he'd come back. She frowned and rubbed her temples.

Every inch of her body ached from the accident, but the physical pain had nothing on the torment inside her. Her life was changing, and as far as she could see, it was all going downhill.

How could she trust herself to get behind the wheel again? Especially with Owen in tow? She couldn't. Terror overwhelmed her at the mere thought of driving.

Which presented yet another problem. How could she *not* drive without raising Zachary's suspicion? Once he left—and she knew he would soon—what would she do? How long would Joshua stick around this time? She'd meant what she said to Zachary about helping Joshua change, but with each day that passed, her conviction that he could change went a little more to pot.

She'd been spoiled for the past couple weeks, letting Zachary take Owen to and from school, run errands. Without a big turnaround on Joshua's part, those duties would be her responsibility once again when Zachary left. She couldn't let her great-grandson down.

She should confess to Zachary what was going on with her…only she didn't know what it was. And she was scared to death to figure it out.

No. She couldn't tell her grandson something was wrong with her head. She refused to be the reason his job got screwed up in Wichita. She was supposed to look out for him, not the other way around.

Just then the truck pulled into the driveway. Elsa didn't rise from the table, but she saw Zachary's head pass by the window. And keep on going into the yard.

She stood so she could see where he was going, but he kept walking, out of her view.

The back door opened and Owen entered with a loud greeting. She went to the door, not only to hug him but to see what Zachary was up to.

What the devil was he doing in the Salinger backyard talking to Lindsey? Probably apologizing for the inconvenience his senile granny had caused her yesterday. The girl had been helpful, reassuring. And having her take Owen away had been a godsend. He didn't need to witness his great-grandma losing it.

THE DAY AFTER HER FAUX PAS with Zach, Lindsey's schedule was screwy—she'd had an early morning meeting and had two evening appointments—so she didn't feel bad about taking a long lunch hour to finish the shoveling.

Her muscles whimpered after she'd been at it for close to an hour. She was almost done, thank goodness. Never again would she choose exercise over convenience.

"Hey, Salinger!"

Lindsey frowned at the sound of Zach's voice and automatically glanced toward the house to see if her dad was lurking. He wasn't.

The voice came from the backyard. She walked a few steps to look around the edge of the house. Zach stood on the property line and when he saw her, he gestured to her to come over.

She shouldn't. But she did.

"What's up?" She tried so hard to keep her voice indifferent and uninterested.

Their eyes met and he glanced at her lips, as if remembering her stupid move yesterday. Except it didn't look like he considered it a stupid move, judging by the flash of interest in his eyes. That one glance was enough to heat her blood.

"I wanted to say thanks."

Thanks? For kissing him? "Why?"

"You went out of your way to help us. I'm sure your dad didn't take kindly to it."

Lindsey, get your mind off the kiss.

"It wasn't a problem." Small lie on so many levels. "I like Owen. He's a great kid."

Zach nodded. "I also meant with my grandma. I, uh, didn't handle things too well."

"Oh. You're welcome. You were upset. She knows. I was just relieved she didn't take my head off."

Zach laughed. "You're not so bad, you know that?"

"Thanks, I think."

"Sure would make things easier if you were."

He turned and walked away, leaving her to wonder what he meant.

ZACHARY TURNED AND TRUDGED back through the snowy yards toward Elsa, and she ducked her head inside.

"How was your day?" she asked Owen.

"We had recess inside!" Which apparently translated into a good day. "We played Duck Duck Goose and a hiding game."

Elsa listened as the boy rattled off the details before he wandered into the living room to his box of Hot Wheels. Zachary came inside, stomping off his boots on the door frame.

"Hey, Gram."

"When did you get so friendly with the Salingers?" She didn't mean to sound so harsh.

The guilty look on his face would've made her chuckle if she'd been in a better state of mind.

"I wouldn't call it friendly, really. I thanked Lindsey for her help."

"Now that I think about it, you two were mighty familiar with each other yesterday. Something going on with the Salinger girl I should know about?"

Zachary wouldn't meet her eyes, which made her grin.

"Not what you think." He removed his jacket and draped it over a chair as was his habit—always had been. He sat at the table and she followed suit. Taking a deep breath, he leaned his elbows on the table but still avoided eye contact. "Lindsey's the reason I came back to town in the first place."

He caught her off guard, but she kept any sign of it from her face.

"She called me after she found Owen outside by himself. She was…worried."

Elsa frowned. This wasn't going at all where she'd expected. "What was she concerned about?" As if she couldn't figure it out.

"You. She thought maybe you were having problems. Was surprised to find Josh gone and you in charge."

"Who was surprised to find me gone?" Joshua stood in the doorway. Clearly, he'd just woken up.

"Sit down," Zach told him. "You're part of this."

"Doesn't sound like something I want to be involved in." He ambled over and sat, anyway.

Nervously, Elsa brushed away nonexistent crumbs on the table. "I've been responsible for kids plenty of times before. You two included." She couldn't help being defensive.

"I know, Gram. I know. I told her she was off base."

"But you rushed home."

"I came to Lone Oak to make sure she understood not to mess with us."

"Who are we talking about here?" Joshua asked.

"Lindsey." Zach motioned toward the Salinger house.

"You came home to check on me," Elsa said.

He faced her. "Well, yeah. I didn't believe you were having trouble, but I had to make sure."

Zachary's voice wavered, and Elsa knew he'd changed his mind. Why had she gotten in that car yesterday? She'd had a spell earlier in the day and while she'd recovered from it, she obviously hadn't been up for driving. She didn't know what to say. Waited in fear for him to speak instead.

"Gram."

She leaned on the table like a school child who knew she deserved punishment. The moment of truth was here. No matter how strong her instinct to fight it.

"I'm starting to think Lindsey might be right," Zachary said.

"Who the hell is listening to her?"

Joshua demanded angrily. "She doesn't know a thing about us."

Elsa ignored him.

She'd lose her freedom. Have a babysitter hovering over her all the time. Be the talk of the town, the entertainment for the week.

It felt like a physical blow squeezed the air right out of her lungs. She couldn't swallow, couldn't get enough oxygen in. Pressure built behind her eyes. She talked herself through a couple of breaths. In. Out.

"I'm starting to think she might be right, too," she said quietly.

She didn't glance at Zachary but she could feel his stare.

"That's crazy, Gram. You're just fine." Joshua had never handled problems well. His confidence in her was nice, but she was afraid it was misplaced this time.

Zachary leaned toward her and awkwardly touched her twisted old fingers. "What's going on, Gram? You've got to tell me everything."

The pressure turned to tears. She never used to be such a baby. Closing her eyes, she nodded.

Tears fell and wandered down her cheeks, but it was no more mortifying than admitting to her grandsons she was losing her mind.

"I have…spells, I guess. I forget what I'm doing, where I'm going. Sometimes forget names. Faces."

He didn't look entirely surprised. "How long has this been going on?"

She pulled her hand from Zachary's to support her forehead, elbow on the table. "Several months."

"Since Christmas? When I was here then?"

"It's gotten…worse lately."

"You've never seen any problems?" Zachary asked Joshua.

"I haven't been here much."

"And when you're here, you're drunk."

"Go to hell."

"Boys." Her head was pounding.

Joshua stood and stomped out of the room. She heard the television click on. She hated to think it, but it was probably just as well right now. He didn't seem in the mood to be useful.

Zachary turned back to her, thoughtful.

Not condescending as she'd expected. "Yesterday?" he asked. "Was that one of your spells?"

"The wreck wasn't, no. But I'd had one earlier."

He hopped up and dug through one of the drawers for the phone book. She tried to ignore him as he flipped through the yellow pages. While she was relieved the truth was out, she dreaded the future. Things weren't going to get any better, only worse. She could feel it in her old bones.

Zachary slammed the skinny phone book shut, frustrated. "I'll call Dr. Fletcher to get a referral. I think it's time we go to a specialist." He returned to sit beside her. "It'll be okay, Gram. We'll get it figured out."

The sadness in his expression nearly did her in. All she could do was nod and look away. She knew it wouldn't be okay.

CHAPTER TWELVE

AS SOON AS OWEN AND GRAM were in bed and Josh had disappeared for the night yet again, Zach grabbed a beer from the fridge and headed out to the shop. He hadn't had much time since he'd been home, but tonight he was drawn there, troubled, like so many nights when he was younger.

There was a sharp bite to the air but he'd left his coat inside. The sky was moonless, so it was a struggle to find the keyhole.

At last, the door opened into the chilly room. Without hitting the light switch, he crossed to the far side. The side facing the Salinger house.

The lights on their lower level were on, but he didn't see anyone on the back porch. Yet.

He needed to see Lindsey tonight.

Grandma's admission this afternoon had thrown him. Sure, he'd finally realized something might be wrong with her but to have her lay it all out for him.... She was scared. That was something Zach hadn't witnessed before, and it scared him, too.

Zach raised the blinds and turned on the light. He hoped she'd see him and drop by, even though he had no reason to think she would. It'd been years since she'd come here.

Zach paced, turned the heat up, thought about lighting a fire. He found himself at the window again, squinting into the darkness.

This was stupid. He'd never *needed* to talk to Lindsey before. There was no reason to start now. Lots of reasons not to.

He went to the row of cabinets that had once served as the kitchen of the in-laws quarters. Rummaging through one of the drawers, he found a stack of old notebooks, some with sketches of projects. He pulled out a blank one and forced himself to settle on the couch against the opposite wall, even though settling went against every fiber of his being tonight.

After ten minutes of sketching a design he hadn't realized he wanted to sketch, he popped up off the couch and turned the light out. Strode to the window again and looked for a sign of life on the Salinger porch.

She'd obviously outgrown her spying habit, just when he needed her.

Frustrated, Zach headed out the door.

As he neared the Salinger back porch, he glanced at his watch in the light from the window. It was after nine. Her old man would probably be in bed by now.

Zach tapped lightly on the back door. He didn't even know what he wanted to say to Lindsey. He just knew she might make him feel better. He didn't stop to think how dangerous that was.

When the door opened, it was Mr. Salinger standing there, scowling at him. He was supposed to be in bed.

"Is Lindsey here?"

"It's too late for visitors."

The door quietly closed in Zach's face. He heard the click of the deadbolt.

It might be late but that wasn't the reason he wasn't allowed to talk to

Lindsey. It shouldn't be any of the old man's business. She was twenty-eight years old, for God's sake.

His instinct was to knock again, but he knew it'd get him nowhere.

Zach left, letting the screen door of the porch slam shut. He returned to the shop and pulled out a small wall shelf he'd made years ago but never finished. At the time, he hadn't been happy with his workmanship, but now he didn't care. He grabbed a piece of sandpaper and went to work on it—a lot harder than necessary.

Half an hour later, he'd sanded the shelf down to nearly nothing and his arm ached. He glanced out at Lindsey's again and saw a light on upstairs. He was simultaneously struck by a memory and an idea.

Was he that desperate? No. Maybe. But it'd be satisfying on several different levels. Somewhere on the list was defying old man Salinger.

Just like he'd done years and years ago, he went into the garage. He cringed when he saw the gaping Buick-sized hole in the back, before grabbing a thick rope.

Minutes later, he was perched on a

branch of the tree closest to Lindsey's bedroom. He took a minute to catch his breath and check out the neighborhood from this vantage point. What was he doing up in a tree? For a woman. Hell, it wasn't for her, it was for him.

That was only slightly more acceptable.

He crept out on the limb as he and Lindsey had done so many years ago, hoping the branch would hold his weight now. It started to bow and he leaped to the roof of the porch with a loud thud. He'd kissed his sanity goodbye.

Carefully, he made his way to her window. The roof creaked under his weight. The shade was drawn so he couldn't be sure Lindsey was the one inside. Might as well find out.

Zach tapped his knuckle on the glass and waited. He strained to hear anything inside. The light went off and his heart pounded. What was he thinking?

The shade moved, just a crack, and he thought he saw Lindsey peering out at him. Abruptly, the shade went up, startling the crap out of him. She opened the window a crack.

"What are you doing?" she whispered, kneeling.

He smiled. Couldn't help it. He hadn't been bad for a long time. It felt good.

"I wanted to talk to you."

"Right now?"

"Earlier, actually, but your dad wouldn't let me."

Lindsey eased the window up. "It's freezing. Get in here."

Gladly. He climbed in and shut the window behind him as softly as he could. If old man Salinger didn't like him at the back door, he'd hate to see what he'd do with Zach in Lindsey's bedroom.

A chill ran down his spine and he realized exactly how cold it was outside. But looking closely at Lindsey from the light of her laptop shot instant heat through his body and his pulse doubled.

She wore rose-colored silky pajamas— a thin-strapped tank over baggy pants that looked like they'd slide off at nothing. Her long hair was damp and hung down over her shoulders. He longed to brush it back so he could see her face better. So he could touch her.

"You came by earlier?"

"Got the door shut in my face."

"I'm sorry. I must've been in the shower."

He shrugged. She wasn't responsible for her old man's actions. "Aren't you cold?"

"I wasn't until I had to open my window." She went to the closet and stretched up to reach the top shelf. Zach couldn't help noticing how the thin pajama material draped to outline every curve of her ass. She pulled a sweatshirt down and over her head, lifting her hair out. Being alone with her in such a private place, her personal space, made Zach's blood pound so hard he could feel it.

He looked around the room. It was small with a single bed in one corner, a dresser and a desk on the opposite wall. The bed was unmade, the covers bunched halfway down. The pink-and-yellow, floral comforter matched the curtains. The room was awash in femininity, bordering on little girlishness.

A stack of file folders sat near the computer on her desk, the chair askew. "You were working?"

"The paperwork never ends. I have reports to do on two new cases, plus updates on several others." She took a step toward him. "Are you going to tell me why you're here?"

He closed the rest of the distance between them, staring at her unadorned face, her lips. She moistened them with her tongue as if knowing his thoughts were on her mouth.

"I messed up the other night."

Without more of an explanation, without thinking, really, he bent to kiss her.

She was startled at first, but he didn't back off. Deepened the kiss. Lindsey wound her hands around his waist and kissed him back.

She tasted like heaven, all minty and feminine. He wanted to taste the rest of her, touch her, explore every inch of her body.

That'd have to wait, apparently, as she pulled away from him abruptly.

"Zach. You can't do that." She smiled though, and there was the dimple.

He gave into the urge to brush his thumb over it, his other hand still on her side.

"Why can't I?"

"You just...can't." She stepped away from him and their contact was broken. "That's not really why you risked your neck to climb up here, is it?"

He laughed quietly. "Maybe not, but it'd be well worth the risk."

Her grin became self-conscious, and she sat on the edge of her bed. He sat next to her.

"Seriously, Zach, what's going on?"

He forced his thoughts to his grandma and the buzz from kissing her weakened. "You were right about Gram."

A week ago it would've killed him to say that to her but now it was what he needed to do. He wanted her help. Needed her on his side.

"What happened?"

"She admitted something's wrong." He told her about the spells and the forgetfulness. "She's scared to death, Linds."

Lindsey's chest tightened just thinking of what he and his grandma had been through. Worse yet, what they still had to face.

"She's lucky to have you," she said, unable to keep from touching his hand.

"What can I do? You saw how I acted yesterday. I don't know why it gets to me like that."

"She's like a mother to you."

He nodded. "Closest thing I've had to one."

"Did you make an appointment with a neurologist?"

"Dr. Fletcher referred us to one in Topeka. Figured the shorter drive would be better for her."

"Good."

They were both silent for a few minutes, thinking about his grandma's future. "Maybe it's something simple, like a deficiency in a specific nutrient or something," she said.

"Yeah. Maybe." He shook his head. "I don't think so."

"If it turns out to be the worst, we'll get you guys some help. There are support groups, in-home nurses, all kinds of options."

"I'd like to hear more about it if and when the time comes."

She nodded.

He closed his fingers around her hand and smiled. "Thank you."

"For what?"

"I don't know. Understanding, I guess. It's been nasty over there. Josh is in denial. Gram is paralyzed with fear. Owen doesn't know what's going on but he senses something's up. I'm so unqualified to handle all of that...."

"No, you aren't. You're handling it." She squeezed his hand. "I cannot believe you snuck up here." She smiled, thinking how surreal it was to be sitting on her old bed in her dad's house, holding Zach's hand. How against the rules.

Before she could think further, he kissed her again. Ran his fingers through her hair, to the back of her neck and drew her closer to him.

She was fully aware she was being stupid. She'd kissed him two other times ever and he'd turned her away twice. Glutton for punishment.

But Zach was hot. The kiss was good. She wasn't about to stop it now. She knew where she stood with him and didn't expect this to last for longer than it took him to realize he'd done exactly what he didn't mean to do. Carpe diem, baby.

Only he didn't stop. He leaned her back on the bed, moved on top of her and continued to kiss her senseless. Reality faded and all that mattered was the feeling of this man on top of her, his desire for her. Her need for him.

He was gentle yet fervent, somehow selfless and selfish at the same time. He explored her mouth, her neck, the skin right above the neckline of her unsexy sweatshirt with his lips and tongue. Her insides melted and she ran her hands under his shirt, on his bare flesh. She wanted more.

That startled her into caution. "Aren't you supposed to pull back right about now and run off?"

He paused, looked into her eyes. "Huh?"

"Seems to be your way. Any second now you'll realize…something…and remember this isn't supposed to happen. *We're* not supposed to happen."

Zach propped himself up more, still apparently not committed to stopping.

"Owen was in the truck waiting the other night."

"Yeah. But Owen wasn't born thirteen years ago. You know, round one."

"Out back," he said, as if there was any uncertainty which incident she could be referring to.

Lindsey didn't bother to answer.

Zach rolled onto his side, suddenly serious. "What are you saying, exactly?"

"We kiss, you turn me away. What I don't get is why you keep allowing it to start when you have no interest."

"No interest?" He laughed. He rolled onto his back and looked at the ceiling. "You really think that's what happened back then? I had no interest?"

"Seemed like it." She couldn't say more—even her cheeks heated at the memory. Closing her eyes, she tried to escape from that raw feeling of rejection that had seared her then and continued to affect her long afterward.

"Making you leave years ago was one of the hardest things I've ever done." His hand found its way back to her waist, this time beneath two layers of clothes to her bare skin.

She tried to tell herself she didn't want his hands all over her body. Waited for him to explain himself.

A low masculine noise came from his throat, a cross between a groan and a growl. "No interest." He mumbled it to himself like it was a bad joke, shaking his head.

"In my experience, interest usually comes out differently from 'you have to leave.'"

"You had to leave because if you had stayed for another thirty seconds, I would've had a real problem backing off."

"I thought I made it clear I didn't want you to back off." As ill-advised as it had been, it was true. She'd been willing to lose her virginity to him. It hadn't been planned, but she'd felt reckless and carried away.

"Sleeping together would've been a mistake."

"Obviously." She sat up, and he let his hands fall back to his sides.

"I wanted nothing more than to sleep with you that night. To have you come to the shop and practically throw yourself at me…that's what guys dream of."

"I didn't throw myself—"

"You know what I mean. You initiated it."

That was true enough, even if she was ashamed of it now. She waited for him to continue, but he was silent. Frustratingly so. "It was such a dream you couldn't handle it, huh?"

"What could I give you, Lindsey? I was eighteen years old with a bad reputation and no future. What good could possibly have come from us being together that night?"

She had no answer. At the time it'd seemed like stopping was a lot worse than having sex with him.

"I wasn't asking for anything."

"But you deserved more, anyway." He sat up next to her. "Don't kid yourself. If word had gotten out—and no, it wouldn't have been from me—your golden reputation would've been shot."

She stared ahead of her, not seeing anything. Yes, being with Zach would've caused a scandal if anyone had found out. But she hadn't cared at the time.

"Let me get this straight," she said.

"You made me leave for my own good." She didn't buy it. As he'd said, he'd been an eighteen-year-old male.

"Forget it. Believe what you want." He rolled off the bed and stood.

She didn't want him to leave.

Maybe he wasn't lying to her. If he was, wouldn't he keep arguing? But she'd believed for so many years…

"I thought you lost interest because I said you'd be my first."

Zach chuckled, but it echoed hollow, humorless. Then he drew a long breath in through his nose. "If you thought that, you don't know how guys think."

"I was sixteen."

"I promise you…your inexperience made it even harder to stop."

She looked at him, beginning to understand he told the truth. "Harder, huh? Yeah, I definitely remember it was hard."

He narrowed his eyes, then laughed. For real, this time.

"So, if you were looking out for me back then, what about now?" she asked.

"Now you can stick up for yourself. You can make your own decisions."

Though there was a hint of condescension in the whole idea that she couldn't do either back then, she couldn't help but be touched. She'd always sensed he was different. Better than people thought.

In the span of fifteen minutes, the history between them had taken on a completely different meaning, and Lindsey needed time to let it sink in. Yes, she could make her own decisions, and while the thought of snuggling back into Zach and seeing where things went was tempting, she decided to stop while the stopping was…possible.

Besides…holy crap. Her dad was just downstairs. What was she thinking?

She stood next to him. "Thanks for telling me that. And as much as I'd like to have you stay so I can get a bad reputation, I think it's best if you go."

He leaned forward and kissed her. She gave in to the temptation, but the hotter the kiss became, the more aware she was of where they were. If she and Zach finally did, after all these years, make love, she wanted to savor every second of it, not worry about keeping quiet or being caught. She pulled away.

"One of these days," he whispered huskily.

They stared into each other's eyes for a long beat, and his intensity nearly knocked her backward a step. He was serious. The invitation was clear.

She tried to smile, then retreated to the other side of the room. "I can see if my dad's asleep and let you go out the front door."

"What fun would that be?"

She grinned and moved toward the window. "Figured you'd say that. Don't fall off the roof and break your neck."

Zach lifted the window wide enough to easily fit through and climbed out. Before leaving, he ran his fingers along her jaw, making her shiver with desire. "See you soon."

As he headed toward the branch, Lindsey shut the window quietly and closed the shade. She didn't care to witness him falling to his death tonight.

ZACH HEADED BACK TO the shop. He was too keyed up to go to bed. Besides, he didn't want to think. Too many feelings to deal with and he didn't do feelings very well. Not if he had a choice. Working with his hands always helped him forget.

He stared at the sketch he'd made earlier and decided it wasn't half-bad. He looked through the supply of scrap wood he still had out here, taking inventory. He didn't have everything he needed to build a hutch but he had enough to get started. He grabbed a couple of one-by-sixes.

Sliding his protective goggles down over his eyes, he turned the electric sander on—his arm was still screaming from the earlier manual sanding—and tried to drown out any thoughts about the silky-haired princess who'd felt so good. He'd convinced himself he was succeeding when the door swung open and Josh stumbled in.

Zach shut off the sander. His brother made a hunched beeline for the couch and collapsed.

"Skunked again?"

As if there was any question.

Josh lifted his ball cap to try to focus on Zach, then placed it back on his head, low, so it covered his eyes.

His brother was never going to learn. Zach had tried to be patient, tried to give Josh time to figure it out on his own, but he just continued to drink. He walked over to the couch and flicked Josh's hat with his fingers. Not surprisingly, Josh's reflexes failed him.

"What?"

"Get off my couch."

"Since when is it yours?" He slowly sat up and put his hat on right.

"What are we going to do?"

"'Bout what?"

Zach clenched his jaw and looked away. He was done with this game. "Get your butt in the shower and sober up. Then we're going to talk."

Josh stood, swayed, then made a great effort not to stumble to the small bathroom. Zach was surprised he went so willingly. Surprised but relieved. He wasn't up for kicking his brother's ass tonight. If he got started, he didn't know if he could stop.

Twenty minutes later, Zach was on the verge of pounding the door down when the water finally shut off. Josh emerged looking slightly steadier and not quite as glazed.

"What's up, man?" He looked unperturbed as he sat back on the couch.

Zach leaned against the wall and crossed his arms. "You have to stop drinking."

Josh's gaze moved downward to the old braided rug. "I know. I was—am. I…" He stared at the floor for several seconds. Ran his hand from his forehead to his chin. "I…don't think I can." His voice was so quiet Zach barely heard him.

Zach had come to that conclusion a while back, but still…hearing Josh voice it was a blow. An alcoholic brother. Fatherhood was out of the question until he sobered up. "We need to get you some help."

Josh stood and paced. "I don't know…"

"Do you enjoy living like this?"

Josh didn't look at him, but he didn't protest, either.

"You could do it, you know. We'll help."

Josh looked shaky, as if he might be sick. He lowered himself to the arm of the couch, grasping his thighs for support. Zach sat a couple feet from him.

"Owen's a great kid, Josh. He deserves stability. Think what he's been through."

Sweat appeared on Josh's skin. Good.

He'd made all the arguments a dozen times, so this time he tried silence.

Josh labored up off the couch and took a few steps. "Okay, I'll go to a meeting or something. Just give me a few days to get used to the idea."

"A few days. In the meantime, you've got to be home more often. Sober."

His brother nodded, still looking green. "Gram's thing…the spells…it just set me off. I didn't know what to do."

So he drank.

"You're not the only one with the problem. We'll get you help."

So a neurologist for Gram and an AA meeting for Josh. The next few days were going to be a jolly time.

LINDSEY'S ABILITY TO concentrate on work had flown out the window with Zach, so she figured she might as well try to sleep. *Try* being the key word.

Two hours later she still lay there. Her mind churned, her emotions spun like a tornado.

Zach had cared enough years ago to

"protect" her…it was overwhelming. Misguided, maybe, but that wasn't the point.

All these years she'd believed she hadn't been good enough, experienced enough for him, but he'd seen it the other way around. The knowledge made her care even more for him. Which, technically, was a bad thing.

She punched her mattress and gritted her teeth. Of all the men in the world, why the one who made her dad relive his grief on sight?

She did care about Zach. Had for years, even though it'd been necessary to deny it. After tonight, she couldn't lie anymore.

Lovely spot she was in…between the proverbial rock and a hard place. She was torn. She longed to know Zach better, to explore what was between them. He'd awakened such things inside her tonight.…

But her dad. He deserved happiness, not to be reminded of the most painful event of his life.

She could spend time with Zach behind her dad's back, but that would only last for so long. And the joy would be diminished by the guilt she seemed unable to escape.

She was in a no-win situation, period. For the first time, she was no longer sure which side she wanted to fight for.

CHAPTER THIRTEEN

ZACH WAS UNACCUSTOMED TO all the approving smiles he was getting from old ladies and young moms alike. He imagined they made quite a domestic picture to anyone who didn't know better—he and Lindsey sitting together at the fast-food table while Owen and Billy, the six-year-old from the group home, played in the giant jungle gym. No one here, on the outskirts of Topeka, knew a thing about his last name or his history. Just like in Wichita.

He watched Lindsey, on her feet now, coaching the boys above as they crawled through a tube. They wanted to get to the blue slide—not the red one or the yellow one—and couldn't find the way through the maze.

Lindsey could direct *him* any day. His gaze stuck to her backside, her cream-colored slacks hugging her legs and her snug shirt revealing every curve. She was something else, enjoying every second of interaction with the boys. Unlike the mom to their left, who held a paperback and glared any time her children interrupted her reading.

The boys finally found the blue slide, as evidenced by their hundred-decibel hollers going down it. Lindsey made her way back to their table.

She sat next to him without a word, her gaze seeking out the boys again as they raced to one of the ladders to re-enter the tubes. Zach looked more closely at her. Her eyes looked damp. What the…?

"Linds?"

She turned to him and smiled. Then she reached for his hand. "Thank you."

"For?"

"Coming with us today. Bringing Owen." She'd invited them to a model train show in Topeka, hoping Owen and Billy would hit it off. They had—they'd both had a blast running from one train setup to the next. "I don't think Billy has ever had so much fun before."

It *was* a tear and it was about to fall.

"Lindsey, are you crying?"

She laughed and wiped her eyes. "Sorry. Sappy girl alert. I'm just happy Billy and Owen are getting along. They act like they've been best friends since they were born."

"And you're crying about it." Zach smiled and shook his head, sliding his arm around her and dragging her closer to his side. "You're nuts, you know that?"

"You don't know how much Billy needed this. The group home is a lot better than living with his mom, but he isn't making any friends." She wiped her eyes again and sniffed. "So, thanks."

"Been a real hardship, spending time with his knockout guardian."

"Not a guardian. Just trying to be a friend to him."

"This isn't official duty?"

She shook her head. "I wanted to get him out and about. Give him something to get his mind off his troubles for a while."

He studied her for a long moment. "It's more than a job to you."

"What do you mean?" Lindsey asked as

she picked up her cup for a swig of caffeine.

"Your job. It's not just a job."

"If you're asking whether I care beyond a paycheck, of course. How could I not?"

That much was clear. She was such a better person than he was, and she was thanking *him?* His reasons for going had been completely selfish, without a thought for the kid who'd recently been removed from his home.

"Uncle Zach!"

He looked up to see Owen and Billy mashing their faces against a window in one of the tubes. Chuckling, he waved.

"So what's Billy's story?"

The smile left Lindsey's face. "His mom needs drug rehab among other things, but she doesn't seem to think she has a problem. She threatened him, hit him, abused him verbally…it's amazing he's still so upbeat and trusting."

"He doesn't seem like a troubled kid."

"That's one reason I want to find him a permanent family quickly, before he loses his naiveté. It's a lot harder to get through to them later."

"How can you be sure a family's going to be better for a kid?"

"What do you mean?"

"How do you know the adoptive parents aren't going to be screwups, too?"

She looked at him closely—too closely.

"Most of the time, just having someone with a good heart who cares what happens to the child is a huge improvement," she said. "But we screen families very carefully. I'd never let any of my kids go to someone I had a bad feeling about."

Lindsey rested her hand on his thigh, and he fought not to imagine that hand roving. She was so much more relaxed with him here, far away from the possibility of having one of her dad's friends walk in and recognize her—and him. Zach could almost imagine they were a couple with no history between their families. He could almost pretend he actually had a chance with her.

Chance or not, Zach had started to figure out so much more about Lindsey today. He could understand now that she would try every last thing for Owen before taking him from his family, just like she would for all her other cases. He suspected her heart was broken every time she had to resort to such a decision.

He could even understand why she thought he was a good solution for Owen, although he wouldn't say that out loud. Even Zach, with all his weaknesses and no experience with kids, was a better answer than living among strangers or being put into a group home.

He had a lot of thinking to do about Owen's future. A large part of it would depend on whether Josh took their conversation seriously or not. So far it'd been four days and Josh had been home a lot more. Sober, as far as he could tell. Whether he'd been sneaking drinks or not, Zach didn't know, but he wasn't being blatant about it. Josh had also been trying to interact with Owen. Zach could tell his brother was genuinely scared of doing the wrong thing for his son. It was enough to keep Zach's hopes up.

"We should probably go soon," he said finally.

Lindsey nodded but made no move to get up. Zach didn't want to budge, either.

They watched the boys for several more minutes before she finally stood. Together, they convinced the boys to come down so they could drive home.

Later, Lindsey pulled the Civic into the Rundle driveway. They'd already dropped off Billy, and Owen was sound asleep in his booster. Zach wasn't ready for the night to end, but with Owen he had no choice. He wasn't sure Lindsey felt the same, anyway. She'd made him leave her bedroom the other night when all he'd wanted was…

Reluctantly, he climbed out.

"I'll get his booster seat," Lindsey whispered.

Zach awkwardly lifted Owen and wedged them both through the car door opening that wasn't made for a six-foot-two man carrying a child. Lindsey picked up Owen's seat and closed the door softly. She followed Zach to the front porch. He held the key out beneath Owen's leg, and Lindsey unlocked the door for them. She set the booster just inside, said good night and left, even though Zach was dying to kiss her.

The house was dark and quiet. Gram must be asleep. Josh was either in bed or gone again. Zach didn't want to guess.

He went straight up to Owen's bedroom without turning on the light and put the boy on his bed. As he slid Owen's shoes off, the child stirred.

"Uncle Zach." His eyes fluttered shut again as he smiled. Zach grinned, too. "Today was my favorite day ever."

"I'm glad, buddy. I had fun, too."

"We always have fun together. I love you the most of anybody."

Zach nearly swallowed his tongue and lowered himself to the mattress. Fortunately Owen drifted back to sleep immediately, so there was no need to find his voice.

He meant to get up and recover from Owen's declaration in the privacy of the guest room, but he couldn't pull himself away. He sat there watching Owen sleep. Held his hand. The corners of Owen's mouth tipped upward even as he slept.

Overwhelmed, Zach finally stood and snuck out of the room. On the way down the hall, he noticed Josh's door was closed. He opened it and was shocked to see his brother already asleep. It was early...usually Josh was just getting ready to tie one on about now. Maybe he really was dedicated to sobering up. Zach was afraid to hope.

"How 'bout a round of ice cream on me?" Wendell Salinger and Mrs. Hale walked behind the rest of the group— Lindsey, Katie, and Savannah and Michael, and their kids.

The children both cheered.

Allie's basketball team had just won a game. Katie had driven home for a long weekend and had made a point of arriving in time for the game.

Mrs. Hale had often gone to Lindsey's and her sisters' events, but this was the first time she'd joined them for a grandchild's game. Lindsay's dad hadn't been out of the house more than a handful of times since his heart attack. Mrs. Hale held on to his arm.

"Are you sure you're up for it, Dad?" Lindsey asked.

"'Course I am. Doctor said I'm healed."

"He's a big boy, Linds. If he wants to treat…" Savannah shrugged.

"Let her obsess," Katie said lightly. "She's good at it."

"You just tell us if you get tired."

"You're mollycoddling," Savannah said so only Lindsey could hear.

"Yeah, well, you know me."

"He's fine now. Let him get his life back."

Lindsey couldn't help worrying about him.

Ten minutes later, they'd pushed two tables together and crowded around them, relatively quiet as they went after their ice cream like lions for a side of zebra.

Lindsey looked at her dad as he finished the last bite of his banana split and tossed his napkin in the paper boat. He tapped his fingers on the table nervously, and her internal radar went on alert. Something was up.

When Mrs. Hale finished her single cone, his eyebrows rose in question and Mrs. Hale nodded subtly. Lindsey leaned forward.

"Kids, we have some news. Claudia and I are getting hitched."

Katie set her half-empty sundae cup down. "Hitched?"

Lindsey reached across the table and squeezed her dad's and Mrs. Hale's hands. "Congratulations! I thought you might be heading this way." They'd been spending even more time together since Mrs. Hale had returned from her trip. Lindsey had been glad to get back to her own home. She'd never been big on third-wheeling.

A glance toward Savannah told Lindsey she wasn't surprised by the news, either. "I've been wondering if you were ever going to make your move, Dad." Savannah grinned as she finished her ice cream. "Mrs. Hale, are you sure you're up for this guy?"

She smiled widely. "I believe I am. And you girls should call me Claudia now, don't you think?"

"Hear that kids?" Michael said, leaning over to pat his father-in-law on the back. "Grandpa's getting married."

Logan's eyes got wide and Lindsey guessed he didn't understand. Allie wore a huge smile. "Can I be a flower girl?"

"That's Claudia's job to figure out,"

Lindsey's dad responded with a wink at his granddaughter.

Katie wasn't smiling. "When did this come about?"

Their dad chuckled. "Well, it wasn't overnight, that's for sure. It's been building for a long time. Neither of us had the nerve to speak up. Then Claudia had to leave for so damn long, and we were both miserable."

"I told you you were grumpy," Lindsey teased. "He was unbearable."

"We ran up quite a long distance bill," Mrs. Hale said. "It's so good to be back home where I belong."

Katie stirred her melting ice cream. She'd always been the most protective of their mother's memory. In fact, she'd come home this weekend to take their dad to the cemetery on the anniversary of their mom's death. It'd always been Katie's job to go with him. Savannah preferred to go in private, and Lindsey just plain didn't go.

Lindsey reached out and touched Katie's shoulder, giving her a sympathetic look. If this was what their dad wanted, Lindsey was thrilled for him, but she felt just as sympathetic of Katie's position. It'd take her a while to get used to it. In the end, though, she was sure their dad's happiness was all any of them really wanted.

CHAPTER FOURTEEN

THE MORNING OF MARCH TWELFTH dawned gray and cold. Just as dreary a day as the one thirteen years ago.

The night Zach had grown up. That sounded dramatic but it was true. The night Josh had smashed into Lindsey's car and killed her mother instantly.

The date had always bothered Zach. He'd tried to put it out of his mind each year, but it seemed he always had to write a check or fill out the date on a bid or a contract. And it never failed to scream out at him like the death sentence it was for Mrs. Salinger.

This year, ignoring it was even more impossible since he was right next door to the Salingers. Seeing Lindsey's car pull up at her dad's midmorning didn't help. The housekeeper had returned, and Lindsey had moved back to her own place a few days ago. Her absence hit Zach harder than he'd like to admit. She visited her dad frequently, but it was usually in the evenings unlike today.

Today must be awful for her.

He tried to concentrate on work. Even though Chuck had given him leave, Zach was adamant about being involved in the next meeting with the commission. He had more to research before they met again, but he found himself reading information three or four times without absorbing any of it.

He played Hot Wheels with Owen, discussed the local bone-headed county government with Gram, paced to the dining room window repeatedly.

"Zachary, what in the devil is wrong with you today?" Gram asked.

It was early afternoon, and Zach still couldn't sit still. He lowered himself into the overstuffed chair. Gram sat in her recliner trying to do the crossword puzzle from this week's newspaper. Zach had figured out how to tell when she was having a bad day—she didn't even attempt a puzzle then.

"Thirteen years today." He was intentionally cryptic because Owen was on the living room floor building a garage for his cars out of Lego blocks.

"Thirteen years what?" Gram squinted thoughtfully, then nodded as understanding dawned. "The accident."

Sometimes her mind was so clear he could let himself believe she was absolutely fine. But he'd taken her to the neurologist and the doctor had shown plenty of concern. They'd get her results from a whole battery of tests soon.

Neither of them spoke for a couple of minutes, but Gram put her puzzle aside. "Wonder if it still bothers your brother."

Josh was out in the driveway working on his truck. Sober. Zach imagined he didn't give that night much thought.

"It was the point of no return for him," she continued, seeming to speak more to herself than to Zach. "He's never made it back." Gram shook her head sadly.

Zach was more worried about how Lindsey must feel.

"She's not so bad," Gram said, still lost in her own world.

"Who?"

"Lindsey. She likes to take charge. But she's good with him." Gram nodded toward Owen, who appeared to be ignoring their conversation.

"What makes you bring her up?"

"She's on your mind, isn't she? That's why you keep looking in that direction?"

"Didn't know I was," Zach lied, ignoring the other question.

"I think she's all right." Gram watched him closely when she said it. "Must be a tough day for her."

Gram seemed content with the mostly one-sided discussion so far, so Zach remained silent. When restlessness finally drove him to stand, he paced toward the dining room window again. Old man Salinger's car was pulling out of the driveway, with Wendell in the passenger seat. Zach strained to see if Lindsey was with him. A woman drove—an older one. The housekeeper. Another was in the backseat, but her hair was too light. Katie, he'd bet.

Which meant Lindsey was probably by herself over there.

He almost wished he hadn't seen the car leave, because there was no way in hell he'd venture over to check on her with her father home. But now he knew. He was itching to see her.

He sauntered back through the living room toward the kitchen, trying to appear unaffected.

"Zachary."

He looked at his grandma.

"If you want to talk to her, go talk to her. I'm not going to stop you."

"Talk to who?" Owen apparently was listening.

"Lindsey," Zach answered, considering what would happen if he did go over to see her.

"Can I come?" Owen asked.

"No," they both answered at the same time.

"Not today, O."

Shrugging, Zach decided to do it. She may not be happy to see him, but he was going to wear a path on the carpet here if he didn't do something. He grabbed his coat and went out the back door into the frigid air.

Zach headed straight through the back porch to the door and knocked.

He waited for her to answer, and the longer he waited, the more he started to wonder if someone besides Lindsey was there.

Finally the door opened. Lindsey stood there staring at him. She was covered in flour.

"Hi," he said awkwardly. "Are you by yourself?"

She smiled—too brightly. "Yeah." She backed up so he could get by her, then shut the blasted cold out. "What are you doing here? What if my dad was home?"

"Nice to see you, too." Being reminded that her dad considered him bad news was getting old. "I saw him leave a few minutes ago, otherwise I wouldn't have come."

Her shoulders relaxed. "Thanks."

She went back to the kitchen counter, which was covered with clutter—baking ingredients, measuring cups, bowls. A radio played upbeat music.

"What are you doing?" He leaned against the counter, confused that she was acting so…normal. Today.

256 THE BOY NEXT DOOR

"Baking. Cookies, cake, bread."

"I didn't know you baked."

"I don't very often. I guess I'm kind of manic about it. I figure if I'm going to mess up the kitchen, I might as well mess it up good. Want to help?"

"I don't know a thing about it."

"Come over here."

She grasped him by his elbow and steered him in front of a big bowl. He looked down at the sleeves of his dark brown leather jacket and frowned at the white handprints.

"Can I take my coat off?"

She laughed and slid it off him from behind. Sadly, that's all she removed.

She set his jacket on one of the kitchen chairs, then parked herself in front of a different mixing bowl. She measured out ingredients and threw them together as if she'd forgotten he was there. Finally, she looked up at him.

"Well?" she said.

"What am I supposed to do?"

She leaned over and ran her finger down a recipe he hadn't spotted. "I've only got the butter and sugar in there so far. Just go down the list—most everything's out here on the counter for you. Measure, follow the directions."

He'd never baked before, but he figured it was best not to mention that now.

He picked up the recipe card for Salinger Chocolate Chip Cookies and read through every word. Okay, he could do this. He started measuring, wondering how to bring up the topic of her mom or if he even should.

"You never told me why you're here."

Nice opening. "Do you know what day it is?"

"Saturday."

He thought her reply sounded almost flippant, but he couldn't gauge her mood. "The date."

Lindsey faltered. "Yeah. I know." She resumed mixing the stuff in the bowl. "They say it's supposed to snow tonight."

Maybe she wasn't as okay as she wanted him to think.

Zach concentrated on adding ingredients before he tried again. "Doesn't it get to you?"

"No." She licked some batter from her

thumb, then poured the contents of the bowl into a cake pan. "I don't let it. It's just another day."

"How can it be?"

"It just…is. I don't like to wallow because of what the calendar says."

Noble. But he wasn't sure he bought it. "Have you been to the cemetery today?"

"My dad's there now."

"What about you?"

Lindsey put the cake pan in the oven and set the timer. She shook her head. "I don't like cemeteries."

"No one likes cemeteries." He measured chocolate chips and dumped them in the bowl. "You really don't go?"

"I don't see what good it would do. It won't bring her back."

He was stunned. Lindsey was doing a bang-up job of hiding her feelings—from him *and* herself. He shouldn't care. He should be glad she wasn't suffering.

They measured and stirred in silence for several minutes.

"It's always gotten to me," he said.

Lindsey's spoon clattered to the floor. She didn't immediately pick it up. "What has?"

"March twelfth."

She stared at him for a long moment, then bent to retrieve the renegade spoon. She threw it into the sink, pulled another out of the drawer and went back to mixing the hell out of whatever was in the bowl.

He was sure of it now. The date bugged her, too. Whoever said that men were the insensitive, uncommunicative gender had never met Lindsey.

"You have nothing to say to that?" he asked.

"What do you want me to say, Zach? I'm sorry it bothers you. I really am. Don't hold it against me that it doesn't bother me."

For not being bothered, she was sure defensive.

It was stupid for him to be here. He'd come over to comfort her and she didn't need comforting. Didn't want it.

So be it.

As soon as the cookies were mixed and ready to drop onto the baking sheet, he washed his hands.

"I need to go."

"Yeah, my dad should be home soon."

Her dad was all that mattered to her.

He went to the door, but before opening it, he paused. "I think you're scared to visit her grave."

"No, I'm not."

"Every time the subject's brought up, you change it to something else. Anything else." He stared at her. "I wish I could help somehow."

He went outside and closed the door before she could tell him again how fine she was.

He felt edgier now than he had before.

As he reached his grandma's back door, he heard a car and turned to see Lindsey's dad pulling into the garage. He almost wished the geezer had shown up five minutes earlier. Then what would Lindsey have done?

DAMN HIM!

Lindsey dropped spoonfuls of cookie dough onto the baking sheet. Flung them down, actually.

It was no business of Zach's whether she went to the horrible cemetery or not. Visiting a grave was a dumb practice, one she'd never subscribed to. It was a stone with a name on it. It wasn't her mom.

The back door opened and Katie, their dad and Claudia walked in, all of them red-eyed and quiet.

"Hi," Lindsey said. "The first cookies should be done in about fifteen minutes." She hated that they all seemed lost in a fog of gloom. *That* was why she didn't go with them.

"Thanks, honey. I'm going to rest," her dad said.

On top of the grief, he looked exhausted. He still wasn't used to leaving the house. His face was pale and his eyes drooped. He shuffled off to his room.

Katie dropped her purse on the table. "I'm going to change and go for a run." She hurried out of the kitchen.

Claudia removed her coat and sat at the table.

"Thanks for going with them," Lindsey said. It was something Claudia had always done. She'd worked for the family since long before Lindsey's mom had died.

"Of course." Claudia bent down to remove her boots, then set them on the mat by the door. She watched Lindsey for a minute. "You don't seem as cheery as when we left."

Lindsey considered telling her about Zach's visit. It was her dad who was so against the Rundles. She had a feeling Claudia was much more relaxed in her opinion of them, although she'd never express it openly.

Lindsey glanced over her shoulder to make sure they were alone. "Zach came over. I'm not sure why."

"Zach Rundle?" Claudia kept her voice as low as Lindsey's. "I didn't know you two were so friendly."

"We're not," she lied. "I guess he wanted to tell me I'm awful for not visiting my mother's grave."

Claudia didn't respond. That made Lindsey wonder if she, too, thought Lindsey was a bad person.

"He said I'm scared to go to the cemetery."

"Are you?"

She glanced quickly at the woman. What was with everyone today? She hadn't gone in the thirteen years since her mother had died and *now* she was in cahoots with the devil?

"I honor my mom every day. She's the reason I went into social work."

"Lindsey." Claudia's voice was kind. "You don't have to defend yourself. Everyone handles things differently." She patted Lindsey's arm affectionately before leaving the room.

Lindsey couldn't help wondering if the woman had really meant, "I know you can't handle thinking about your mother's death." Which was true.

She finished the cookies, baked two kinds of quick bread and frosted the cake after it cooled. Finally, with the help of some good music and the busy work of baking, she didn't feel compelled to knock the daylights out of anyone who so much as mentioned her mom.

As Claudia had said, everyone handled things differently, and this had been Lindsey's way of handling it for the past thirteen years. She was just fine the way she was, thank you.

CHAPTER FIFTEEN

OKAY, SO LINDSEY WASN'T quite "just fine." She was lonely and avoiding going home. Doing her best not to think about the significance of March the twelfth.

Now that Claudia was back, her dad didn't need her as much. He didn't even complain very often about not being able to go into work full-time yet, now that he was in for half days.

After they'd debated for over an hour about the future of small-town newspapers and what effect the Internet would have on them, he'd finally given up and gone to bed, back in his old bedroom upstairs. Claudia had checked in to her private suite early as well. Lindsey didn't know if the separate bedrooms were for appearance sake or not. She didn't want to know. However, she'd left the kitchen light on to signal she hadn't left yet.

The house was too quiet. Lindsey did so well during the day, even when Zach had come sniffing around to see how she was holding up. Daytime was easier, when there was a lot to keep her busy. But now, she didn't have the energy to do much of anything.

She'd thrown on a jacket and gravitated to her favorite place on the back porch. Something about the darkness and the night air, and even the crisp temperature, made her relax.

It had absolutely nothing to do with the fact that the light was on in Zach's shop. Yeah. Right.

The blinds were open, and she remembered his revelation that he'd always kept them raised on her account. That he liked having her watch him.

Was he sending her a message? An invitation?

Attempting not to look at the lighted window was a joke. Her eyes were attracted to it like a man to a thong bikini.

He moved in and out of her line of sight.

A chambray shirt hung from his shoulders, unbuttoned to reveal a plain white tee beneath. He wore his usual faded blue jeans. She was riveted to his movements around the room, getting tools out, searching through wood scraps.

She wasn't close enough to see the look on his face, but he paused in what he was doing and ran his hand through his hair. He stared thoughtfully at the table in front of him. Then, as if he sensed her, he looked directly at her.

Surely he couldn't see her from there. She tried to write it off as coincidence.

Heck if she could sit there and wonder any longer. She checked inside to make sure her dad was sleeping, made obvious by the snoring she could hear from the top of the stairs—so much for the love life she'd imagined for him.

Lindsey slipped out the back door. She shut it without a sound, hurried across the wooden porch floor and descended two steps to the crunchy, icy lawn.

What was she doing? The last time she'd snuck over to see Zach in the shop, she'd come away angry and embarrassed.

After kissing him and coming darn close to taking off all her clothes for him.

Things had changed since then, of course. She was no longer a naive, inexperienced high school girl. He'd made it clear she was welcome. And that was the bigger danger.

She pressed forward, telling herself it was because she couldn't stand being alone tonight. She just wanted to get away from the silence.

The windowless door of the stone shop was on the opposite side from her dad's house. As she reached the corner, she turned back to make sure no lights had come on inside. Nothing.

Blowing her breath out in a cloud of steam, she knocked gently. The door opened seconds later, as if he'd been waiting for her, and judging by the lack of surprise on his face when he saw her, he probably had been.

A slow smile crawled across his face. That smile did things to her that shouldn't be legal.

"Wondered if you'd be by," he said.

The cocky jerk.

Raising her chin a notch, she played back. "I saw you looking for me."

He stepped closer. "You did, huh? And you still came over?"

A spark of mischief in his eyes made her catch her breath, but she refused to back away. She wasn't afraid of him. She was afraid of herself.

Looking over his shoulder, she asked, "What are you working on?"

The room looked much the same as it had years ago. The far half was dedicated to woodworking, with different saws and other tools, as well as a large workbench. A hooded light loomed over the area but wasn't turned on, leaving the room blanketed in the soft glow of a single lamp near the sofa and a fire in the fireplace.

An ugly blue-and-green-plaid couch stretched along the wall to her left. Ah, yes, she remembered that couch. On the wall to her right hung an electronic dartboard she hadn't noticed before. She hadn't noticed much besides Zach the last time she'd been here.

"A surprise for Gram. A new hutch for all her collections of dishes. For a woman without a lot of money, she's got a load of dishes. They're stuffed away in her closet."

She was touched, once again, by his thoughtfulness toward his grandmother.

"She'll love it." She moved around him toward the work table. "What's it going to look like?"

He joined her at the table and his male smell filled her nostrils. No cologne, just man. He picked up a pad of paper and showed her detailed sketches of a hutch.

"Did you design that yourself?"

He nodded and pointed out several features.

Lindsey didn't want to show she was impressed. He'd just think it was grounds to kiss her or some other stupid thing.

"Care for a drink?" he asked.

This was too familiar. It was exactly how the evening had begun thirteen years ago. He'd offered her a beer and she'd accepted. Alcohol hadn't played much of a part in her advancing on him that night, but still…

"No, thanks. I just had something at my dad's."

Grabbing the notebook with the plans, he crossed to the fridge and took out a Sprite. Then he lowered himself to the sofa. "Can I get your opinion on something?"

She started toward him but the open blinds beckoned to her. All her dad had to do was wake up and look out the window. "Mind if I close these first?"

He gave her a mischievous look and she rolled her eyes.

"My dad has a weak heart. It's better if he doesn't know I'm here."

"Feel free."

Oddly, his cockiness made her want to throw him off balance by kissing him instead of shying away, as he probably expected her to do. The thought tantalized her as she reached up to lower the blinds, then shrugged off her coat.

She walked to the couch but sat on the arm of it instead of next to him.

This could be fun. But also dangerous, she reminded herself. It'd be best just to give him the opinion he asked for and keep a safe distance from that body, which screamed muscles and lust.

"What kind of opinion do you need?"

Suddenly, he was all business. "Down here at the bottom, I could either leave the shelves open, put on glass doors, or use solid ones so the space is hidden. What do you think?"

"Solid doors so she can hide stuff."

He chuckled. "You have a lot to hide, do you?"

Their eyes met and neither looked away. He was smiling.

"I'm an open book," she told him. "But then, I don't collect dishes."

"I don't think you're as open as you like to pretend." His tone became serious, his words pointed.

She stood and took a few steps away. "I think your grandmother would appreciate some covered storage space. It wouldn't be good for displaying so close to the floor, anyway." She turned to see him staring at her, and her temperature climbed by several degrees under the weight of his gaze.

Zach nodded and made a note on the plans before setting them aside. Lindsey scanned the room for the darts she knew lurked somewhere. When she turned again, he stood inches away from her and she could feel his body heat.

"Why'd you come over tonight?" he asked in a low voice.

He was too close. She could see the individual threads in his shirt, the muscular chest below it.

"Darts," she blurted.

"You came over for darts?"

Getting a hold of herself, she took a step back. "Yeah. Darts. Where are they?"

"In the cabinet," he said, gesturing toward the dartboard. "You any good?"

"Not really," she lied. "Wanna play?"

THIRTY-FIVE MINUTES LATER, the game was over. Lindsey flopped down on the sofa, disappointed that she'd lost, even if it was by a hair.

Zach sat a couple feet from her, shaking his head. "'Not really good,' my ass." She'd led the whole game, but a lucky triple nineteen at the end had saved him.

"What are you complaining about? You won."

"Barely. You would've nailed the three your next turn."

"Probably." She grinned.

He crossed his left ankle over his right knee. "You try to come across as such an open book, but that's not the case at all, is it?"

Lindsey stiffened. "Why do you say that? Since I got here that's your second reference to me being secretive."

Zach debated silently whether to get into the topic that'd bothered him all day. The truth was he'd rather climb to her end of the sofa and kiss her senseless, but he suspected that'd be the easy way out. For both of them.

He wasn't feeling particularly easy tonight.

"Your secret dart talent isn't the only thing you're keeping to yourself."

"What else, oh, Wise Guy?"

"I still don't believe today doesn't get to you."

Her eyes narrowed slightly. "Would you rather have me whimpering around all day? Why can't I be okay?"

"*I'm* not okay today. I didn't know her that well. She wasn't my mom." He leaned his head on the couch. "Lindsey, every year when this day comes around, I get knocked flat by memories of that night."

"Just because you're bothered, you think I should be, too?" Her voice wavered on the last word, just enough for him to know she wasn't as unaffected as she wanted him to believe.

"It has nothing to do with me. I just think it doesn't add up that you're fine."

She stared straight ahead in silence.

"That night changed my life, Linds." She still didn't look his way. "Up to then, I was out to raise hell. People thought I was bad news, well, I'd show them bad news. Josh and I were alike that way."

For a moment, he considered shutting up, but he suspected that was the problem. Everyone else had shut up about it, too. If she ended up hating him after tonight, well, then…nothing much had changed.

"I heard the crash even though I was inside the house with all the windows closed. It was that loud. The kind of sound you just know something horrible has happened."

She squeezed her eyes shut.

"I knew right away it was Josh. Knew

it like I knew my own name. I tore up the street and could see it from the corner. Saw his pickup. Couldn't make out the other car yet. Didn't even consider it much because I was just thinking about Josh. Then I got to the scene."

He stopped talking, the lump in his throat swelling. Lindsey had drawn her knees up in front of her and hugged them. Tears streamed down her cheeks and Zach felt like the worst kind of jerk.

Sliding closer to her on the cushions, he resisted the urge to take her hand. He had a point to make. "One of the worst things is that I saw you, Lindsey. I saw you as you got out of the car. The horror in your eyes…. It rocked me to the core. In that one instant, I understood how much pain being 'bad news' could cause."

He could no longer *not* pull her to him. Somewhere in his brain he registered surprise when she reached for him at the same time.

Burying her face in his chest, she wept into his T-shirt. He held on to her tightly, suspecting this would do her good but wishing now he'd kept his mouth shut.

"Let it out," he whispered, though he wasn't sure she could hear him between her gasps for breath.

"Damn you." Her words slashed at him. She fought for control—he could see it on her face. "You don't understand."

Taking her with him, he lay back on the couch, settling her alongside him. She let him do it. Rested her head on his chest where her tears had soaked him.

"You're right. I don't."

Her breathing deepened and she didn't respond.

"Why can't you talk about it?" He understood what it was like to avoid talking, but that's not what this was. She could normally keep up with the best.

She breathed in deeply and closed her eyes. "I begged my mom to go to a movie that night," she said hoarsely. "She didn't want to go at all, didn't want to get out in the cold, didn't want to see the movie I did, didn't feel like going, period. I talked her into it."

"Sounds like you two were close."

Her eyes popped open and she glared at him. "You don't get it. I forced her to go when she wanted to stay home and watch *NYPD Blue* with my dad."

His throat tightened as he realized belatedly where she was going with this. "You didn't force her, Lindsey. She made up her own mind."

He felt her shake her head against him. "That's not the only thing." She paused, and the seconds stretched out. "I was driving the car, Zach." Her voice was oddly hollow, barely familiar to his ears.

"I know," he said quietly.

She plastered her face into his shirt again. *"I was driving."*

He squeezed his eyes closed. "No. Lindsey, no. Don't do this. The accident was not your fault."

Her silence told him she wasn't convinced.

"My brother was tanked. He ran a stop sign and broadsided the passenger side of your car. Open and shut case."

She sat up and hugged her knees again, facing away from him. "Easy for you to say."

This was far beyond anything he knew how to help. Who was he kidding? He didn't know how to help a blasted thing. Shouldn't have ever brought up the subject in the first place. But the need to get it out in the open between them, to tell her his part of the story, how he'd been affected, had driven him.

The more she talked, though, the more he understood—the way the accident had changed him...was *nothing*.

"A drunk driver hit you, Lindsey. He broke a laundry list of laws."

"I don't expect you to understand, Zach. I hear you, and in my head, you make sense. But it's not getting through any farther. Inside here, I regret every second of that night." She clenched her fist to her chest.

Lindsey felt like she exhaled for the first time in an hour. Zach tugged her back down against him, and she acquiesced, sure she'd never felt so wiped out. There was a reason—okay, a host of reasons—she didn't let herself think too hard about the night her mother was killed. Number one, she couldn't bear the crushing pain.

"Lindsey—"

"I don't want to talk about it anymore."

He studied her, looked as if he was about to lay into her, but then he didn't. She needed silence and, wisely, he gave in. The only sound in the room was the faint ticking of an alarm clock.

Beneath her head, his chest rose and fell, and she allowed her hand to rest on it. His hand was on her waist, and his thumb caressed her, back and forth, in a soothing motion.

Lindsey closed her eyes and shut out the pain. She simply listened to Zach's breathing. Felt the sturdiness of his body. Took in his smell, the familiar masculinity with a hint of detergent lingering in his T-shirt. If she concentrated only on the man beside her, everything was okay.

Zach wasn't usually one for lying still, doing nothing, but he couldn't remember when he'd been as content as he was now, with Lindsey stretched out against him. She'd seemed to cry some of her sadness out. Not that he expected miracles.

With each minute that ticked by, Zach lost more ground in the battle not to notice how she felt as a woman. The silkiness of her hair draping over his arm and shoulder. The inward curve of her waist and the thin strip of exposed skin under his fingers. The faint floral scent that teased his senses.

Her breathing became slow and even as she dozed off. He reached up to the lamp on the end table by his head and switched it off, leaving only the flickering glow of the fire.

That Lindsey trusted him enough to lower her guard and fall asleep struck him somewhere deep inside. He was a jerk for putting her through the hell of remembering. She'd have been much better off if she'd run away.

Several minutes later, she stirred, running her hand over his chest and crossing her leg over both of his. The sigh that escaped her as she shifted made his blood pound in his ears.

Just as he thought she was going back to sleep, she raised her head and opened her eyes to look at him. A half smile pulled at her lips.

"Have a nice nap?" His voice sounded strained.

"Mmm." Her contented response curled around him.

His smile was forced, as he was no longer sure he had any control over himself should she make the smallest movement in any direction. He wanted to kiss those lips, to take that mouth, to taste her, devour her. But he couldn't do it. Wouldn't let himself.

Thank the Lord God above, he didn't have to.

She crept up his body until their mouths were even. When she gazed into his eyes for a long beat, he could tell she was second-guessing herself and he held his breath. In the next moment, her lips were on his, light and tentative, and he said a second prayer of thanks.

Funny how lust could make a man religious.

In seconds, the kiss went from gentle and caring to probing and selfish. Which suited him fine. Lindsey centered her body over his, with a knee on each side of his legs. She dug her hands through his hair as if she couldn't get close enough to him. In his mind, she couldn't.

Lindsey knew she should probably slow down, back off…think about what she was doing. But that was the point. She didn't want to think, anymore. Didn't want to feel anything but what Zach's roving hands were making her feel. She wanted to forget the memories that had been dredged up, escape the vulnerability that came with the pain.

Forgetting the past was easy when she draped herself across Zach's tempting body, her long hair falling over him, closing out the world. Heat shot through her and centered low in her abdomen. At this moment, she didn't care what her dad would say if he found out. She didn't care about history. All she cared about was that Zach could turn her inside out.

Her breathing was uneven. So was his, she noticed with satisfaction. She pulled her head back enough to look at him, to reassure herself this was really the man she'd had a thing for since…nearly as long as she could remember.

"Good morning," he said, even though it couldn't be much past midnight.

"I'd say." She could stand to wake up to him every day.

"So…are you going to leave again?" he asked in a husky voice.

"Are you going to send me away again?"

"Do I look crazy?"

"I was hoping you'd say that." She traced his lips with her finger.

She basked in his intoxicated lust. His half-closed eyes. Dazed grin. The contradiction between the hard lines of his jaw and the soft, tender way he touched her. She shivered. She was finally as close to him as she'd always wanted to be. Or almost. So far, it was even better than she'd imagined to feel his arms around her and his muscled chest below her. Her heart pounded as she leaned forward to take exactly what she wanted from this man. Tonight, that was everything. She put the ramifications completely out of her mind as she kissed him again.

CHAPTER SIXTEEN

LINDSEY STRADDLED ZACH ON THE couch, loving the hardness beneath his jeans that touched her right where she needed to be touched.

There were too many layers between them. She wanted his clothes off so she could touch every inch of that body, taste it, admire it. Sitting up, she inched his T-shirt toward his neck, trailing kisses from his tight abdomen up over his chest, whisking over his nipples with her tongue and eliciting a catch in his breath. He sat up and removed his shirt the rest of the way, then switched to hers.

"Did you wear a shirt with a jillion tiny buttons on purpose?" he growled.

"All part of the plan to make you crazy." She loved seeing the desire in his eyes, hearing it in his voice.

Lindsey watched impatiently for a few seconds as he eventually unfastened the top few buttons. "There's a secret to it," she said, gently moving his hands out of her way. She kissed him slowly, thoroughly, then lifted the shirt over her head and threw it on the floor.

"I like the way you think."

His hands moved to her breasts, cupping the weight of them, then he skimmed his thumbs over the thin material of her bra. She leaned into him, aching for more.

"I suspected all along you were attracted to my brain," she said breathlessly.

"If that's what you thought, then you haven't seen your backside sway from side to side when you walk."

He sat up and took possession of her lips once again, running one hand through her hair, dragging her head closer and slipping the other beneath the satin to her breast.

At his touch, a moan escaped from Lindsey but she barely noticed. She was too focused on feeling more of him. She moved her fingers over his bare skin, and her touch seemed to have a similar effect on him.

Zach had held himself back for too long. He couldn't get enough of Lindsey, her smooth flesh and surprising passion. She seemed almost reckless.

He reached behind her and unfastened the scrap of material that remained between them, wanting to touch her all over. She arched toward him. Reclining her backward, he lowered himself on top of her and took her nipple in his mouth.

Her hands dipped below his waistline into his jeans, and he rose enough for her to unzip the fly. She reached inside, freeing him from the confinement of his clothing. The first contact of her fingers on him made him bite his lip.

He had to remind himself not to rip her clothes off and take what he wanted so badly. Not yet. Not with Lindsey. He wanted to do this right, slowly, making it last, sending her sky-high with need.

When she slid his jeans and briefs down, ran her hands over his body, he just wanted her naked. Now.

"Lindsey," he said in a rough voice,

trying to put on the brakes long enough to ask a question. "Oh, God," he said as she wrapped her hand around him.

"Yes?" she said, a smug grin on her face.

"Are you sure this is what you want? Because we're cruising real close to that line..."

She let out a low, sexy laugh. "You said it yourself...I'm not the naive girl I was last time. I know what I'm doing."

"I'll say." A little too much, if he was going to last longer than a New York minute.

They shed the rest of their clothes, and Zach took in the sight of her body in the dim, flickering light. She was as hot as he'd always dreamed of. Hotter.

"Zach."

Trailing kisses down her jaw to her neck, he muttered a response.

"Do you have something?" she asked.

He pulled away and looked at her until understanding dawned. "Something." He glanced at his jeans strewn on the floor. God, please let him have *something*. "I think I might."

He rummaged for his wallet and dragged out a single condom from one of the pockets. Squinting at the faint date on the edge, he stifled a goofy grin when he saw it was, in fact, still good. He held it up to show her.

Lindsey took the condom, opened it and slid it on him. Her touch nearly drove him over the edge. She urged him closer, but he didn't need to be urged. He pushed inside her and stilled, overcome by the connection that pulsed between them.

He'd fantasized about this moment forever, long before they'd even kissed years ago. Dreaming of making love to Lindsey had always made him weak with desire.

The reality was a hundred times more powerful.

Contrary to his intentions, there was nothing slow or gentle about this—couldn't have been if his life depended on it. Lindsey was just as much behind the driving tempo as he was, meeting every thrust.

Everything else faded into nothing, and Zach was only aware of the two of them and the way they moved as one. He'd never felt so close to anyone, so lost in another person. He gritted his teeth and fought not to lose it until Lindsey did, but it was hard to stay in control. Just as he was about to surrender the battle, she tensed and gasped his name several times. The sound of it on her lips was the most erotic thing he'd ever heard, and it would've put him out of the game even if he hadn't been anywhere close.

As his blood slowly returned to the rest of his body, he sought out Lindsey's lips, unwilling to let the moment end. He felt her shudder a couple more times and smiled. Couldn't stop smiling, actually.

He rolled to his side, taking her with him, not wanting to let go of her. Lindsey made a sexy, contented sound and Zach was nearly ready to go again. When she shivered, he reached for the blanket draped over the back of the couch and pulled it over them.

"I knew it," he said, still waiting for his breathing and heart rate to slow down. "You do hide things."

"What?" Her voice was drowsy.

"You come across as such a good girl." He moaned deep in his throat and kissed her on the temple.

Lindsey grinned. "I *am* good."

Zach could only laugh and think how true that was. Good in bed. Good with kids. All-around good. Too good for him, but he didn't care right now. Nothing was going to spoil this moment.

THE COLD WIND WAS LIKE a slap in the face, snapping Lindsey out of the warm contentment she'd felt in Zach's arms.

Back to reality.

Back to her dad's disapproval of her... lover.

What was she doing? This was crazy. Her heart pounded as she walked slowly through the backyards. The windows were completely dark, which gave her only a tiny measure of comfort. If he was up and wanted to see what she was doing, he'd have all the lights off, anyway.

She couldn't go inside, not at this hour. Besides, she looked like she'd been, well, rolling around with a man. She fought off a smile at the thought of the things she and

Zach had done. On the one hand, guilt ate at Lindsey. Yet she didn't want to completely lose the high she was on, the high caused by the feelings Zach had evoked.

With her fingers crossed, she whipped around the corner of her dad's house, onto the driveway. She hurried down it and made a beeline for her car. Thank goodness she'd parked in front of the neighbor's house. Her dad would still be able to hear the engine if he was awake, but at least it wasn't right outside his window.

She felt like a thief in the night. It wasn't supposed to be like this. But she'd known letting her guard down with Zach would result in a barrage of guilt. At the time it hadn't mattered one bit.

After climbing into her car, she shut the door quietly and eased away from the curb, wondering how she would ever look her dad in the eye.

LINDSEY FIGURED SHE'D TURNED manic-depressive overnight. She'd woken up light and happy this morning. Her body still tingled from loving Zach.

Once she'd stepped into the shower and had become really alert, though, a bone-deep sadness had overcome her. It wasn't just that she'd betrayed her dad. That was horrible enough, but a wrenching sorrow for her mother hung over her, overwhelmed her whenever she let her guard down. It was as though talking about her last night had unleashed the memories Lindsey had held back for so long. She'd lost the power to block them out.

For most of the day, Lindsey had hidden away in her bedroom and buried herself in reports and paperwork for her job. By midafternoon, she'd joined Brooke for a fluffy chick flick in the living room, but even one of her favorite movies couldn't get her off the emotional seesaw.

It was so ironic that she'd found a man who could make her float one minute and be weighted down by guilt and sadness the next.

If she had her way, she'd avoid her dad for a good week or two just so she wouldn't have to look him in the face. But she knew if she cancelled—the whole clan was gathering for dinner at his house this evening—he'd suspect something was wrong. She never cancelled on her father.

She dragged her feet for as long as she could and finally drove to her dad's. As she walked up the driveway, she avoided looking toward the Rundles'. She wanted nothing more than to see Zach, to talk to him, reassure herself the connection they'd formed last night still hummed between them. She wanted to float some more. But she couldn't let herself. Not here or now. It'd be tough enough to act normal around her family as it was.

She walked into the kitchen just as Savannah's daughter, Allie, was setting the table. It wasn't like Lindsey to show up this late. Too late to help Claudia prep the meal. She could swear her dad looked at her funny. No, it was just her guilty conscience.

After suffering through dinner, Lindsey escaped to the front living room. The chatter was getting to her, and for once she didn't have much to add.

She gravitated to the piano—specifically, to the framed picture of her mother with Lindsey and her sisters. The picture had been there since before her mom's death. Lindsey didn't usually pay much attention to it. She was so used to seeing it, she'd become blind to it.

Not tonight.

Her mother was so young in the picture. In her late thirties. Far too young to die. But it had been taken no more than a year or two before the accident. They'd given it to their dad for Father's Day one year.

Elizabeth Salinger had been proud as could be of her three children, and it showed in the picture. Her smile wasn't fake. She looked natural, beautiful, happy.

Lindsey closed her eyes and held the photo to her chest as her throat swelled with sadness.

"Yesterday still bothering you?" Her dad's voice startled her, and she set the photo back on top of the piano.

"No more than usual," she lied, as she walked back toward the kitchen. If he only knew the other things she was keeping from him.

CHAPTER SEVENTEEN

ZACH STOPPED IN SHOCK WHEN he reached the bottom of the stairs. Owen and Josh were on the living-room floor together, working on a Spider-Man jigsaw puzzle. Instead of making a big deal about it, he walked past them into the kitchen.

"What prompted that?" he asked his grandma, pointing over his shoulder.

"Not sure. Maybe it's a good sign."

He liked to think so. "Of course, just when we need to leave for Topeka, they start bonding."

Today was the day Gram would get her test results. They'd decided to keep Owen home from school and take him with them since they wouldn't be able to make it back in time to pick him up.

Zach was trying to stay positive about

the appointment, refusing to believe it could be anything incurable or otherwise bad. Regular aging got his vote for the cause of Gram's spells, or so he kept re- minding himself.

He glanced at his watch. "O, get your shoes on. We need to leave."

"Where are we going?"

"Topeka."

"To the train show?"

Zach grinned. "To the hospital for Gram's appointment."

When Owen didn't budge, Zach walked into the living room to get him going.

"I don't wanna go to the hospital. It's boring."

That was a new word from Owen.

"You can bring a couple toys to play with."

"Please, can I stay home?"

"He can stay with me," Josh said.

Zach's first instinct was to say no, but Josh caught his eye. There was a challenge in his brother's look, an unspoken, *Are you going to give me a chance or not?*

He'd stayed sober for close to a week. That was saying a whole lot.

"Will you be okay here with your daddy, O?"

"Yeah." The boy's attention was back on the puzzle.

Zach moved closer to Josh. "You sure, man? You can handle it?"

"Forget it. You don't trust me."

"I didn't say that. I just want to make sure you're comfortable with it. We'll be gone for three or four hours."

Josh shrugged as if to say it was no big deal.

"Really? You want to do this?"

"Go on," Josh said. "We'll be fine."

Zach hesitated. He wanted to trust his brother, but it'd be better to start with a shorter trip. An hour or so. But if they did that, they might never get the chance. Josh and Owen needed to get used to each other. Both of them were willing right now. He wasn't going to get any better opportunity to let Josh prove himself.

He nodded. "I'll have my cell phone. Call me if you need anything."

"We won't. We're just going to hang out, right, Owen?"

The boy was busy trying to fit two pieces together. "Yeah," he said absently.

All right, then. Owen was comfortable with it, as was Josh. Zach could live with that. This was the first step to getting Josh into full-time fatherhood.

THE CAB OF ZACH'S TRUCK was silent, save for the noise of the engine as he and Gram drove back toward Lone Oak.

What was there to say?

Gram's diagnosis had left no room for small talk, and the thoughts that were likely on both their minds seemed too big, too ugly to utter.

The doctor couldn't say with one hundred percent certainty that Gram had Alzheimer's, but it was *probable*. They could only pinpoint the diagnosis after she died. Zach shuddered at the thought. There'd be a lot of hell between now and then. He could tell Gram was scared. That scared the piss out of him because Gram didn't scare easily.

There wasn't much positive to take from their appointment today. Nothing good they could say about the future, no hope they could offer. Just a downhill road that might last a long time. There was no way to know.

He glanced at her, wishing he could say something that would help. She stared out the windshield, not blinking.

His throat tightened, and he watched on the road ahead as well. He couldn't bear to think about what Gram faced. Or what he faced when she was gone. There was no way to hide from the fact that she wasn't going to live forever, and what time she had left would be painful for everyone.

Zach shivered and turned up the heat. It was a nasty cold day, and the bad news just made it all the more bleak.

His cell phone rang, startling him. He glanced at the caller ID and saw Gram's home number.

"Hey, what's up?" he answered, knowing it had to be Josh.

"You gotta get home, man. Owen took off."

Zach's chest tightened and his mouth went dry. "What do you mean he took off?"

"He's gone. I looked everywhere."

"How long has he been gone? What happened?"

Josh didn't answer immediately. "Look, just get here. I need to go search the neighborhood again."

"We'll be there in less than an hour. Go find him."

Zach hit the accelerator, grateful the highway was clear, even though there was a dusting of snow everywhere else. Snow. Cold. It wouldn't take long for Owen to freeze if he was outside by himself somewhere. He explained what he knew to Gram, hating to worry her but there was no way around it. She didn't say a word, just swallowed hard and paled.

All he could do was drive like a crazed man. And one other thing. He dialed Information and waited for them to connect the call.

Lindsey answered her office line on the first ring.

"Owen's gone."

"What do you mean?"

"Josh stayed with him while I took Gram to Topeka. Owen apparently disappeared. I don't know."

"Oh, my God, how long has he been gone?"

"I don't know. Josh wouldn't say much. He's heading out to search the neighborhood. I'm forty minutes away."

"I have an appointment in twenty minutes and one right after that. It'll be two hours at least. There's no way I can cancel on these people. These meetings are critical."

"Do what you need to do. I'll get there as soon as I can. Maybe he'll turn up by then."

"Keep me posted, Zach. Please. I'll try to get done early."

"How can I keep you posted if you're in meetings?"

"Leave messages at this number. I check them constantly."

"Okay. Thanks, Linds."

"He'll turn up, Zach. He'll be okay."

"Hope you're right."

He hung up, feeling no better than he had five minutes ago. He couldn't ask Lindsey to help Josh look for Owen even if she didn't have meetings. She couldn't be expected to cooperate with Josh no matter what the reason was.

"Interesting," Gram said.

"What?"

"You and that Salinger girl must be mighty close."

"Lindsey, Gram. You know that."

She shot a weighty look at him that he tried to ignore. "We're close," he finally said, unwilling to say another word about it.

"Is this the fastest you can go?" Gram asked.

"We'll get there."

They did, thirty minutes later. Zach went to the passenger door to help Gram down from the truck, but she shooed him away. "Go find him."

He went inside first. The house was empty. He took a quick look around in all the nooks and crannies, thinking maybe Owen had simply outsmarted Josh. No such luck.

On his way out the back door, he noticed Owen's coat wasn't on the hook where it belonged. Maybe Owen had though to bundle up. The temperature was above freezing right now—barely. But when the sun went down this evening…. He had to find Owen before that.

Gram came in, and he ran out, saying, "Stay here in case he comes back."

"Where's Joshua?"

"No idea." He couldn't worry about that right now. Josh would have to take care of himself and hope to hell this wasn't his fault. If it was, Zach might strangle him.

He ran into Josh three houses down, searching under bushes and behind garages. Joining in, he made an effort not to jump down his brother's throat. Yet. "What happened?"

"All my fault, I'm sure. I screwed up. Aren't we all surprised?" His voice was bitter, full of self-loathing, but Zach didn't feel much sympathy for him.

"What'd you do?"

"I lost track of him."

Zach stood up from looking underneath the neighbors' canoe. How did you lose track of a kid like that? He glared at Josh, but his brother didn't notice. Zach was getting more frustrated by the minute. One second Josh seemed worried, the next, he acted like it was no big deal.

He grabbed Josh by the arm.

"What's that for?" Josh said.

"You've been drinking."

Zach could smell it.

"I'm not drunk."

"Only because you can hold more gallons of liquor than the average army brigade." Zach walked off in disgust. His brother had just blown his last goddamn chance.

Half an hour later, Zach was sure Owen wasn't hiding in one of the neighbors' yards. A couple people had come out to help him look. Zach jogged back to his grandma's house, his gut churning.

Not caring what old man Salinger thought, he cut through his backyard, eyeing the barren field behind their houses. It was flat for a ways, but then the land dipped. There were small groves of trees here and there. Places a boy could hide. Zach hoped Owen hadn't trekked through the field and gotten tired. If he didn't keep moving, he'd get too cold, regardless of his coat.

When he got inside, he called the cops, his heart racing. He'd hoped to find Owen tucked under a nearby bush, just as

Lindsey had several weeks ago. But that wasn't the case.

The police got there quickly, and wouldn't you know it, one of the responding officers was Kurt Humphrey. He kept it professional, though, asking more questions than Zach had time for, waiting while Zach searched for a recent picture. Josh didn't show his face. Zach wasn't even sure he was home. Didn't really care. The cops told him they'd scour the neighborhood and surrounding area.

Almost before they'd pulled out of the driveway, Zach hurried to the backyard, heading into the field on foot. He doubted the authorities would get their butts out of their cars and canvass the area yet. If they did hit this field, so much the better. There was a lot of area to cover.

Every step of the way, Zach's anger grew. At himself. At Josh. His brother had always been self-absorbed, but there came a time when you had to put someone else first. When you had a child, for instance.

But Zach was the idiot who'd decided to let Josh stay with Owen for a few hours. That was the biggest mistake of the day.

"THIS IS LINDSEY."

Zach hesitated. "I expected your voice mail."

"I was just about to call you. Any news?"

"The cops found Owen a few minutes ago. He'd made it to Main Street. In his socks and coat. No shoes. He's in an ambulance on his way to the hospital in Layton." More than two hours had passed since Zach and Gram had arrived at home. He'd been about to combust when he'd gotten the call.

"Is he hurt?"

"They suspect frostnip or frostbite, maybe hypothermia setting in, but they think it's mild. They want to check him over thoroughly."

"When are you going?"

"As soon as I hang up. Want me to pick you up?"

"Yes. I can get out of here for the rest of the day, no problem."

"I'll see you in a few minutes, then."

He told Gram he was leaving. She wanted to go with him, but he convinced her she'd had enough excitement for the day. He hurried out to his truck.

Zach and Lindsey collapsed on to the connected chairs that formed a sort of bench in the waiting area.

"Thank goodness he's going to be okay," Lindsey said. She felt as if they'd been in the hospital for twenty-four hours straight, when, in fact, it had been only a few hours.

"Physically, anyway."

She was worried about Owen's state of mind, too, but she didn't need to let Zach know that. He was concerned enough. "We'll get him through it."

According to what Owen had told the police, he'd left the house because Josh had yelled at him for asking him to play cars with him. He was scared of Josh and thought everyone else had deserted him. It sounded like Josh had played with Owen at first before getting irritated and ignoring him. Then he'd apparently laid into the alcohol, or as Owen said, "the bad-smelling drink." Lindsey would never have left him with Josh, but then Zach seemed to have more faith in his brother than she ever would. There was no need to bring it up now. The damage was done, and Zach regretted it like crazy.

"That kid's been through so much the past few months," Zach said. "I told him we were going to Topeka for Gram's appointment. I could've sworn he understood we'd be back in a few hours."

"Kids get confused sometimes. Don't beat yourself up for that. If he was scared of Josh, that just added to his confusion."

Lindsey sighed. She should've picked up on how badly everything was getting to Owen. He'd just seemed so well-adjusted on the surface, and she hadn't bothered to look deeper. That was her *job*. Didn't matter if he was one of her official cases or not.

She glanced at Zach and knew by the look on his face he wasn't cutting himself any slack. She touched his thigh, rested her hand there.

"Can I tell you something?" she asked.

He looked warily at her.

"I've always suspected you have this incredible capacity for caring about people."

He gave a disdainful snort.

"I love it when I'm right." She flashed

a smug grin at him. "Seriously, Zach. I saw a spark of that years ago and I see it now."

Zach wasn't going to deny it. He cared about Gram and about Owen. And this woman next to him who was so intent on... He wasn't sure what she was doing or where she was going with it.

"What you've done for Owen to date is so great. You've made a big difference for him."

"I don't know about that." He'd only done what was necessary to keep her from getting more directly involved. Now he understood having her involved was the best thing that could happen. He was out of his league with Owen and Gram, but Lindsey could talk him through just about anything.

"He loves you. He's bonded with you, Zach. That doesn't always come easy with a five-year-old boy."

"Yeah, well, he loves you, too. If he was older I'd have to worry about him bothering you for a date."

"Ah-ah," she said playfully. "Would you be jealous?"

He wove his fingers with hers. "Darn straight, I would be. I have to give it to him, he knows how to pick women."

"See? He's learning about all kinds of things from you. Women, turkey legs. Stability. Responsibility."

"Stop. You're giving me too much credit."

"That's just it. I'm not." She straightened, her posture signaling to him she was getting serious.

God help him.

"You seem to have some idea that being a good role model is out of your reach."

"I don't know the first thing about being a role model."

"Who does? I told you the other day, a big part of it is simply *wanting* to be good. You do and Owen knows that."

"Linds—"

"I'm not campaigning for you to adopt him right now. You have to make that decision on your own. But whether you do or not, you've already had a positive impact on him. You've been exactly what he needed."

He could almost believe it when she said it. One thing he did know was that she believed what she said. She wasn't a smoke blower. For that alone, he loved her.

Holy shit.

Love was a foreign word.

It had flowed right into his thoughts, though, and there was a reason for it. He was in love with her.

Wasn't that convenient, considering he didn't have a single hope of taking it anywhere? Not when her father couldn't stand the sight of him, and she was all about devotion to her father.

Zach leaned back in the chair, rested his head against the wall and closed his eyes.

There was a reason he didn't do love. Love thoroughly sucked.

He opened his eyes when he sensed someone coming toward them. Unbelievable. It was the woman from the carnival. The one who'd advised Lindsey to stay away from Zach and his family.

She was dressed in scrubs and wore a nametag. Ellen Seamore. Zach squeezed Lindsey's hand, since she had her eyes shut and wasn't aware of the woman's approach.

"Lindsey? Is that you?"

Lindsey and Zach stood. "Mrs. Seamore. How are you?"

"I'm well. What are you doing here?" The woman looked suspiciously at Zach.

"Zach's nephew is under observation for mild hypothermia and frostnip. Thankfully, he's going to be okay."

"I see. And how is your *father?*" Dislike filtered through her words as she studiously ignored Zach.

Lindsey glanced at him. He refused to let the woman know she got to him, and plastered an amused look on his face.

"Um, he's fine, actually. And I'd prefer if you didn't mention you saw me at the hospital…. He'd only worry—you know." Nervously, she looked at Zach again.

Just in case he forgot he wasn't good enough for her, here was his reminder.

"Oh, I see." Ellen's tone was smug.

"We'd better go back and see if we can get into Owen's room," Lindsey said to Zach. She seemed like she wanted to get away from this woman, but Zach knew that was all in the name of keeping her involvement with him from her dad.

Zach turned to see if Mrs. Seamore was

out of hearing range and stopped. "Lindsey, go home."

"What?"

"You don't need to be here. I can handle getting him back on my own."

"I told Owen…."

"I'll tell him you had to leave."

"That's all he needs…one more adult to desert him."

That one cut to the core, even if Zach hadn't abandoned Owen yet. After today, he might not. First things first, he had to get Owen out of the hospital.

"Come on," Lindsey said as she took off down the hall again. She hurried into Owen's room with Zach behind her.

"Hey, Owen. How are you doing?"

"I'm lucky." His grin gave no hint of the day's turmoil.

"You *are* lucky. You could've gotten really sick or hurt being outside for so long," Lindsey said. "I'm glad you're okay. I'd be really sad if anything happened to you, and so would a lot of other people."

The boy frowned as if he didn't believe

her. Lindsey leaned over and hugged him tight. "You're a special kid, Owen."

"I am?"

"You'd better believe it!" She grabbed the stuffed panda bear she'd given him earlier and tucked the bear under the blankets next to Owen. "If you ever need to be reminded how special you are, just hug this guy. He knows you're the best boy in the whole world."

Owen smiled and pulled the bear into his arms. "Okay."

Lindsey glanced up at Zach. She looked as if everything was right in the world. Had she any clue what she did to him every time she put her father's precious feelings before his?

CHAPTER EIGHTEEN

GRAM AND OWEN HAD BOTH GONE to sleep early after their separate ordeals. Josh was nowhere to be found, which was just as well. Zach didn't want to lay eyes on him.

He'd made up his mind earlier, probably the minute he heard Owen was missing.

He was going to adopt Owen.

It would change everything, but he had to do it. He could no longer stand that Owen's future was bouncing around uncertainly, waiting for a bunch of screwed-up adults to give him direction, stability. It was unfair to him.

It was obvious that Josh wasn't going to come through for his son. No matter how much Josh wanted to be in Owen's life, he wanted his liquor more.

So Zach would take Owen back to

Wichita with him soon. After he figured out what to do for Gram.

He was starting to believe he could handle the challenge, that he could do right by Owen. Lindsey had helped him see no one was perfect when it came to parenting—he'd be far from it. But he knew now that he could make a positive impact on Owen. Because he cared a whole lot.

Funny thing, he'd realized at the same time he was also good enough for Lindsey. He'd do just about anything for her and Owen as well.

Too bad it made no difference to Lindsey or her dad.

Zach went out the back door and locked it, headed for the shop. He didn't realize someone was standing at the door until he was mere feet away.

"Miss me?" Lindsey whispered, appearing out of the shadows.

He tried to smile. She looked so good, and he had missed her. But there was no point in saying so. "Like a hangnail." He resisted the urge to touch her. "What are you doing here?" He looked toward her dad's house and noticed a light on.

She shrugged. "Figured it was about time for you to come out to play."

He unlocked the door and she followed him inside. He opted for the low light of the lamp instead of the glaring overhead. "Your dad know you're here?" he asked as he turned it on.

"Hope not," she muttered as she turned away. "Wow, you're almost done with this." She walked over and stood in front of the hutch, which was starting to take shape.

Zach couldn't muster up any interest in his project tonight, so he sat on the high bar stool between the work table and the counter.

Lindsey had sensed something was bugging Zach the second she'd seen him outside. It showed in his posture, in the slowness of his walk. She'd fostered a hope that she could cheer him up, but he was still detached, preoccupied.

After a few one-word responses to her questions about the hutch, she moved toward him, crossing her arms to keep herself from making contact.

"Something's on your mind tonight."

He chuckled. "You could say that."

"What is it? Anything I can help with?"

"Don't I wish."

Lindsey moved to the counter near him and hoisted herself up. She leveled a stare at him and waited for him to explain himself. Of course, he didn't. "Come on, Zach. What's going on?"

He didn't move, just sat there on the stool, legs outstretched, ankles crossed, arms across his chest.

"I'm adopting him."

Lindsey wasn't sure she'd heard right at first. But one look at his face and she knew he was serious. She hopped off the counter and closed the space between them.

"Zach! That's wonderful."

She threw her arms around him awkwardly, but he sat stone still. She backed off. "You're scared."

"Hell, yes, I'm scared. Lindsey, I nearly got him killed today, and now I'm going to be responsible for him full-time?"

"*You* nearly got him killed? I don't think so." The blame belonged to Josh. One hundred percent.

Zach bolted off the stool, away from her. "What was I thinking to leave him with my brother?"

"Probably that your brother would do what he said he would," Lindsey answered, even though he'd posed the question rhetorically.

"Why did I trust him?"

Lindsey leaned against the counter, watching Zach.

"He screws up everything. Why did I think he'd be okay with a five-year-old for several hours?"

"Because he told you he could do it?" Lindsey offered. She knew he'd wanted to believe Josh could handle it all, wanted so badly to see Josh take responsibility for his son.

"His word doesn't mean much, I guess."

Lindsey had trouble arguing with that. "You shouldn't feel guilty, Zach. You made the best decision you could at the time."

"I do feel guilty, dammit. I *am* guilty. Because of me, Owen could've been seriously hurt."

She closed her eyes for a moment,

clenched her fists. He was the one who'd done right by Owen. Had done so for weeks. Zach had put everything on hold for that boy, had acted more like a father than Josh ever would. And yet he stood here full of self-loathing.

"You can't blame yourself for your brother's weaknesses. He's the one who screwed up. Not you."

When Zach didn't flinch or even look at her, she grabbed his arm. "Zach, you have nothing to feel guilty about."

Then he did look at her, so intensely she would've backed away had she not already been against the counter.

"Don't talk to me about unjustified guilt." The coldness in his voice cut her more deeply than if he'd yelled. "When you manage to forgive yourself for your mom's accident, then you can lecture away."

"That's a little different—"

"Bullshit."

"She died, Zach." Tears sprung to her eyes and she wiped them away angrily.

"Yes, she did. And you're going to spend the rest of your life trying to make it up to your dad because you feel like it's your fault."

"If I hadn't begged her to—"

"It wasn't your fault. *You* didn't break the law. *You weren't drunk.*"

"You don't understand."

"You're wrong. I do understand. I get that you feel bad. I get that you regret choosing the night my brother was three sheets to the wind to take your mom to a movie."

"Stop."

"It's been thirteen years, Lindsey. You're still living for your father. You do whatever it is that makes him happy out of some misdirected sympathy and guilt."

"Obviously, you don't know what it's like to be close to a parent." Cruel blow, she knew, but he'd pushed her way beyond any semblance of fairness.

"Maybe I don't. But I do know you're too scared of upsetting your dad to admit you care about me."

Lindsey faltered as guilt over her behavior earlier at the hospital flooded her. "He has a heart condition." Her voice was quiet, unsure.

"So you *do* care?"

He *so* wasn't playing fair. She wasn't in any mood to agree to a thing right now, not when he carried on about how stupid she was to be concerned about her dad. "It doesn't matter, Zach."

"Damn straight it doesn't matter!" He pushed the stool so it crashed on its side. "Nothing matters because there is no future for us. You've never thought I'm good enough for you."

"That's not true, Zach—"

"It sure doesn't matter that I love you, because all you can think about is making Daddy happy. I'm sick to death of sneaking around, sick of being treated like dirt all in the name of pleasing your old man, who hates me."

"You love me?" She'd gotten hung up on that tidbit.

Apparently his big show of emotion was over, though.

"You said it yourself. It doesn't matter."

He ran his fingers through his hair. He looked as if it'd satisfy him more to knock something else over. She watched him in a stupor, still thrown by hearing the *L* word from Zach's mouth. About her.

He fought for control, took a deep breath, closed his eyes. "I know there's no future for us." His volume had lowered considerably. "I've known it since I first laid eyes on you. We were worlds apart then, and it's only gotten worse."

Lindsey didn't know what to say because it was true.

"Go home, Lindsey."

He leaned against the counter again, one hand braced behind him. His shoulders slumped, hair a mess.

She wanted so badly to touch him, but she couldn't. There was no way around it. Staying any longer would only make them both hurt more.

God, did she hurt.

"I'm sorry." Her words were barely more than a hoarse whisper.

Lindsey turned and walked away from Zach for the second time in her life.

THE WIND CHILLED LINDSEY to the bone as she hurried to her car. Tears felt like they froze in the corners of her eyes. She didn't care that she could barely see.

Once inside the Civic, she slammed the

door with all her strength, then made a frustrated growling sound. She started the car and headed home.

On the way, she passed Savannah's house. The lights were on, and Lindsey knew her night-owl sister was still up, wide awake. She could stop and talk, but…no.

She wouldn't know what to say. Didn't know what her problem was. Her dad? Zach? Most likely herself. If she could honestly say she didn't care about Zach, she'd be in a whole different place right now. One that didn't make her eyes burn or her insides knot.

She drove on past, longing for solitude and home.

Brooke was in bed already, as Lindsey had known she would be. Mostly she was relieved. There was no way she could act like nothing was wrong right now, and she sure didn't feel like talking about it.

Fifteen minutes later, she lay in the warm nest of blankets on her bed. But comfort eluded her. She was so out of sorts that home didn't even feel right tonight.

Damn Zach and everything he'd tried to

put in her head! He'd forced her to talk more about her mom in the past week or two than she had in the thirteen years since she'd been killed. But that wasn't even the kicker. The kicker was he'd said he loved her.

Why had he even said that? Zach wasn't the type to throw that word around. She suspected he'd used it rarely if ever. So now, when everything between them came to a head, he put that on the table even as he said they had no future together.

Lindsey, being the sap she was, couldn't just let it drop as she should.

In spite of everything, the pain, the frustration, the anger, Zach had elicited from her tonight, she couldn't help imagining what it would be like to be loved by him.

She hadn't cried herself to sleep for years, but she couldn't stop herself tonight.

CHAPTER NINETEEN

FRIDAY MORNINGS HAD ALWAYS been coffee time at the diner for Lindsey's dad. Today was the first time he'd been able to go since the heart attack. Claudia had a meeting first thing, so Lindsey had insisted on driving him to and from. She worried that the outing would be too much on top of working. He'd grumbled that he wasn't an invalid, but had finally gotten in the car with her two hours ago.

After dropping him off, Lindsey had gone into the office to reckon with several reports that were due and set some appointments. Her day was packed to the hilt, but running her dad home wouldn't set her off schedule too much. Overloaded was good. It gave her no time to think. No time to feel.

She ran out of her office and hopped in

the car, even though the diner was only a block and a half away. Pulling up into a spot right in front, she could see her dad and his cronies at their regular table near the window. Crossing her fingers that he'd come right out, she honked.

The entire table of older men, which included the mayor, the fire chief and several others who ran the town, looked her way and most of them smiled and waved. Thankfully her dad rose—slowly—and spent a couple of minutes heckling the others as he usually did, then made his way to the car.

"You could've come in," he said after closing the door. He sounded cranky, which surprised her. He should've been in a good mood after finally being able to return to his routine.

"I have a meeting so I'm kind of in a hurry."

He took a few seconds to catch his breath, which bothered Lindsey. As he worked on buckling his seat belt, Lindsey spotted something that made her heart drop.

Ellen Seamore walked out of Tut's. Just perfect.

"Did you talk to Mrs. Seamore?" she couldn't help asking.

Seat belt buckled, he met her eyes and she knew before he answered. The woman hadn't been able to resist mentioning she'd seen Lindsey with Zach at the hospital.

"I'm afraid so."

Arguments and explanations flew through her mind, but there was no point. She was the one sneaking around, hiding things. An apology didn't even seem appropriate because, even though she and Zach were officially over, she didn't regret going to the hospital with him. She didn't regret any of her time with him. The only things she regretted were that she'd hurt her dad and that she could no longer be with Zach.

CLAUDIA WAS DUSTING the living room when she heard Wendell come in through the back door. Strangely, Lindsey hadn't accompanied him in as she usually did. She went to the kitchen to see what was going on.

Wendell, who was removing his coat, looked more haggard than usual.

"Are you okay?" she asked.

He attempted a grin. "I'm okay." He walked straight to the table, though, and sat on the closest chair.

"It was too much. You shouldn't have gone for coffee yet. Those men are too raucous." She sat down next to him.

He patted her hand. "Coffee was fine, my dear. Good to be back to it."

"I'm sure the guys were glad to have you."

He shrugged. "I ran into Ellen Seamore. Apparently, she saw Lindsey at the hospital yesterday. With that Rundle."

"Is everyone okay?"

He looked at her in surprise. "I didn't ask. Was too shocked to be conversational."

"You're upset she was there with them."

"Last I knew she was making sure the kid was taken care of. Now she's going on personal family vigils in the hospital with them? How can she do that?"

"She's never been able to turn away from someone in need." Claudia wondered if that was all it was, though. She remembered Lindsey's confession about Zach's visit not so long ago. That'd taken her by surprise at the time, but obviously, there was more going on than she and Wendell realized.

She hoped Wendell could accept that, if and when they were faced with it. Whatever "it" was.

"Ellen said they were close. Familiar with each other. She's been seeing him in secret, I'm almost sure of it."

Claudia frowned. She wanted nothing more than for Lindsey to fall in love and settle down, but she hated to think of the toll it would take on Wendell if it turned out to be Zach she loved.

She was jumping to conclusions. Who knew what was really going on between them?

"What will you do if you find out she cares about Zach?"

Wendell met her eyes wearily. "She wouldn't do that. I don't believe it."

Claudia didn't respond. No need to get him keyed up when she didn't have any solid information, only guesses.

"She knows how I feel about that family."

"Yes. She loves you so much, Wendell.

She wouldn't do anything purposely to hurt you."

He stared at her for several seconds. "There's a 'but' there."

She shook her head. "I don't know."

"You think she's involved with him?"

She considered her answer for a moment before speaking. There was a fine line between preparing him and causing him undue distress. "I don't think it's out of the realm of possibility."

"Hellfire."

"She hasn't confided in me. But I sure wouldn't be shocked to find out there's more between them than the boy."

He stood and paced toward the counter. His back toward her, he paused, hands on hips and raised his face to the ceiling. Her heart tightened at the sight of him so troubled. She laced her fingers through his and rubbed his back with her other hand.

"Let's not jump to any conclusions just yet."

"She couldn't do that. Could she?" He shook his head stubbornly. "I don't believe it."

"One thing to think about. Lindsey has never been the type to date jerks. If she is involved with Zach, we need to try to trust her judgment that he's okay."

He looked at her and grumbled, then went to the refrigerator for a drink. As he sat down at the table again, he pulled the Kansas City newspaper out and turned to the sports section.

In other words, he was done talking about Lindsey and the Rundles.

"I'VE BEEN HOME for three days, and every time you come over here, you're frowning toward the neighbors'," Katie said, seconds after Lindsey had let herself in their dad's front door. Her sister had never been known for beating around the bush.

Lindsey looked around the living room to make sure their dad hadn't overheard.

"You're leaving soon, right?" Lindsey said it in a teasing tone, but she really wasn't in the mood for questions. She'd have to be more careful. She hadn't been aware she'd so much as glanced in that direction. In fact, she made a point of *not* looking for Zach—even though she was dying to see him. She'd come over to her dad's every evening for dinner while Katie was home for spring break, and she hadn't set foot on the back porch. She figured if she forced herself to park in the street, enter through the front door and stay away from the Rundle side of the house, eventually she'd break all the habits she'd developed while sneaking over to Zach late at night.

Sure. And if she held her breath long enough, she'd get out of the habit of breathing, too.

"What's going on with you and Zach?"

"Nothing." Present tense. It was the truth.

"I don't believe you."

Lindsey shrugged and went out to the kitchen. "Where's Dad?"

"Upstairs with Claudia."

Lindsey raised her eyebrows.

Katie laughed. "They're discussing paint colors for the bedrooms. Have they said anything to you about selling the house?"

Lindsey shook her head.

They'd not spoken about much. Of course, Dad was in love. Happy as could be. Oblivious to how much Lindsey was hurting. She was trying really hard not to resent him, but she was losing the battle.

"I hope they hold on to it. Coming home won't be the same if *this* isn't home."

Lindsey nodded half-heartedly, not caring what she was agreeing to.

"Out with it," Katie said sharply.

Startled, Lindsey looked at her sister. "Out with what?"

"Whatever's bugging you. I've watched you mope for three days. It's annoying."

"I'm not moping."

"It's Zach. Fess up."

Lindsey glanced over her shoulder and shook her head. "I can't," she said angrily. Truth be told, instead of feeling better the more time that passed, she felt worse. And the kicker? She was beginning to think she had no one but herself to blame for her unhappiness.

She was gritting her teeth again. She did it so often her jaw ached.

"Let's go talk," Katie said, motioning toward the back porch.

Fresh air might do her some good. Anyway, it was too early for Zach to be in the shop.

"You love him?" Katie shot the question at her before she could even sit down.

Lindsey leveled a stare at her sister. She could deny it. She could tell Katie to leave her alone, tell her it was none of her business.

"Yeah."

She hadn't acknowledged it out loud before. Hadn't let herself think the words. But it was true.

"No way!" Katie leaned forward in her seat. "Lindsey, what are you doing?" Her tone was more excited than upset.

"Absolutely nothing." The monotone of her own voice sounded dead compared to Katie's animation. Fitting, since that was how she felt.

"So. You're in love with one of the bad boys next door, but you can't be with him because of Dad."

"Kind of." Lindsey slumped. "Except Zach's not a bad person. He's adopting his nephew."

A flicker of compassion crossed Katie's face, but then it was gone. She tended to side with their father about the neighbors.

"Does Zach know how you feel?"

"No. He's not going to."

"And that's it? You're just going to let it drop?"

"Yep." Lindsey forced the word past the lump in her throat. What was with her? She'd been walking an emotional tightrope for days, and she hated it.

Thoughts of her mother now haunted her daily. Memories of Zach made her even lonelier. And all the while, the rage built up inside her. She didn't even know what or who she was mad at...just that she felt like lashing out.

"You can't do that, Linds."

"Watch me."

"No. I can't stand it." Katie leaned back in her chair again, tucking one leg underneath her. "Tell me everything. What's happened with you and Zach? I know it's something for you to be so messed up."

Wearily, Lindsey told her all about it.

"He says I won't do or say anything to upset Dad because of my guilt."

"Guilt?"

Ah, great. This was the part Lindsey didn't want to get into. "You were so young when Mom died..."

"I was twelve. I knew what was going on."

"I was driving the car." Lindsey looked hard at her sister.

"Lindsey. Josh was drunk. You weren't to blame!"

"I know that." Lindsey covered her eyes with the pads of her fingers. "My brain knows it. Really."

"But you still feel guilty."

"I still do. I wish I would've challenged her to a game of Monopoly instead of begging her to go to a movie."

"This makes me so mad!" Katie sprang up and paced.

"What?"

"That Josh is still hurting us. Hurting you. He made the mistake, but our family is still paying for it."

In that moment, it made Lindsey mad, too. She hadn't seen it that way before.

"Savannah's always been the rebel," Katie said.

"Huh?" It was true, but where was Katie going with this?

"It's time for you to take a lesson from her."

"Sure. Let me just walk away from Dad forever."

Her sister lowered herself to a different chair. "He's wrong about this."

Lindsey looked at her, surprised.

"Zach's not the one who drove the car. He had nothing to do with it."

"Right," Lindsey said hesitantly.

"You're the levelheaded sister, who makes wise decisions and takes responsibility for everyone and their dog. Dad should be able to step back from things and see you love this guy. If you love Zach, he can't be all bad."

"Yeah. Right. If only it was that easy."

"So take action. Take a stand." Katie popped up again and stood in front of her. She leaned down, bracing her hands on the arms of the chair. "This is your happiness we're talking about! Dad's got his. He'll have a new wife, and he'll still have his oldest daughter tiptoeing around him, bowing to his every need. What are *you* going to have?"

The door to the house opened.

"There you are. Dinner's just about

ready." Claudia smiled and ducked back inside.

Lindsey didn't know what to say to Katie so she headed inside in silence.

"You deserve to be happy, Linds. Just as much as anyone else does." Katie said it just as Lindsey stepped over the threshold, so she couldn't respond. She didn't know what she'd say, anyway.

"I'm such a lucky guy," their dad said as they all helped Claudia get the food on the table. "Another dinner with three beautiful women." He smiled at Claudia.

Lindsey was happy her dad had found someone to love. Really, she was. But she didn't feel like enduring his joy tonight, smiling as if nothing was wrong, when she really wanted to scream.

"Enjoy it while it lasts," Katie said. "I'm taking off tomorrow."

"You're sure we can't talk you out of this latest endeavor?"

"This is just the *class* to learn about storm chasing. It won't be dangerous at all, Daddy."

"I don't like the thought of you running after tornados."

"I'm not. Not this week. Unless we get lucky enough to have stormy weather and get to practice out in the field." Katie's eyes sparkled.

"You're quiet tonight." Their dad watched Lindsey as he spooned rice casserole onto his plate. "Usually you'd be mid-lecture about taking undue risks by now."

"I'm...not feeling well." She stood. "In fact, I think I'll go home."

"I thought my casserole was one of your favorites," Claudia said.

"It is." Definitely wouldn't go down well tonight, though. "I'm sorry. I'm sure it's as good as it always is. I'm just not hungry."

Katie looked knowingly at Lindsey, who offered a weak smile to no one in particular. She pushed her chair back and went to get her coat. "Have a safe trip, Katie."

She hurried out before anyone could say more.

Cold drizzle had her throwing her coat over her shoulders as she rushed to the car. It wasn't dark yet, but it wouldn't be long.

She moved on autopilot.

She was going to the cemetery.

Brooke wasn't home so it took Lindsey less than five minutes to change from her work clothes into jeans and a huge, stretched-out sweatshirt from college. These were her comfort clothes, and she definitely needed comfort tonight.

Before she left, she threw her hair up into a ponytail and pulled her quilted down coat from the closet. More comfort. She had a niggling feeling none of it would be enough.

The cemetery was on the outskirts of town, about a mile from her dad's house. As she turned onto the narrow paved road, the shadows of decades-old trees made dusk seem dark and spooky. She hoped she'd remember where her mother's grave was.

She drove right to the spot where her family had parked thirteen years ago. She remembered the huge elm with the trunk that jutted into the road and the branches that towered over it, giving it the semblence of a tunnel.

Lindsey rummaged through the glove compartment and pulled out a mini flashlight, even though she wouldn't need it quite yet. The light it gave out was dim. It was a small miracle the thing worked at all, it had been stowed so long. Glancing out the wet passenger window at the blurred maze of headstones, she sucked in a deep breath and opened her door.

Beyond the tree and to the north, she remembered. She'd used the fat elm to block her view of the gravesite after the burial service, once she'd finally made her escape.

Here she was, thirteen years later. And she still wanted to escape. Tonight, though, she had a feeling she couldn't run away anymore.

She moved slowly toward the far rows of stones, unsure of what her mother's looked like. It hadn't been there for the burial. Her dad had tried to get her approval of stones and patterns and etchings, but she hadn't paid attention.

She stopped in her tracks when her own last name popped out in front of her. Her chest tightened and the air seemed to abandon her lungs. Taking the last few steps toward it, she read her mother's name and the dates below it. She crouched down and lovingly traced the engraved letters with her finger as if it was her mom she touched.

Tears filled her eyes. Her throat felt like it might swell shut. God, it hurt. Being this close to her mom and yet unable to ever see her again. It was like learning all over again that she'd died. Like she'd been fooling herself for years, telling herself her mom was on a long trip overseas or something. The cold, sleek stone made it all so real. So final.

"Mom," she whispered as the tears poured down her cheeks, indistinguishable from the raindrops.

The dark gray stone disappeared, and all she saw was the accident.

That night had also been wet, except the raindrops had been huge. In the car, they'd looked at each other and laughed.

"So much for hairspray," her mother had said. "Good thing you like me no matter how bad I look."

"I never said I liked you. I just needed a movie date," Lindsey joked.

"Better be a good movie. That rain is cold!"

Lindsey had been so sure it'd be good. She'd been waiting for *Major League II* to come out for months. Baseball and Charlie Sheen, how could you go wrong?

To this day she still had never watched that movie.

Her mom had been happy that night, Lindsey remembered for the first time.

She closed her eyes and let herself see her mom as she'd been then, grinning, wet, smelling of damp hairspray and lipstick.

Lindsey realized she was smiling, and it was bittersweet. She hadn't allowed herself to relive a single second of that night, even the minutes before the wreck. It had been too painful to face.

"I'm so sorry, Mom." She lowered herself to the wet ground. Her sweatshirt and jacket hung low enough to protect her for a while, but frankly, getting soaked was the least of her worries. "If you were here, you'd set me straight." Lindsey's chuckle turned into a sob. "How did I get so screwed up? Everything's gotten twisted around in my head. I miss you so much…."

Lindsey covered her face with both hands and let the sobs come. Minutes ticked by and, still, she cried.

When she could finally take a deep breath without bursting into more sobs, she opened her eyes. Darkness had snuck up on her. She sat closer to the headstone, waiting for the shakes to stop so she could control her body again.

Slumping forward, leaning her arms on her thighs, Lindsey figured she might just have made up for all the years of not crying for her mom. She'd made up for something, anyway. God, she felt wrung out.

She'd always known that her mom's death wasn't her fault. But it seemed as if she'd needed to hold on to the guilt, as if she needed to pay somehow. She hadn't had a reason to give it up before.

Now she did.

She'd always been a fixer, and God forbid she came across something she couldn't fix. Which was exactly what her mom's death had been. Unfixable.

No more.

She loved Zach. Wanted the chance to see where their relationship could go.

Pressure built behind her eyes again as she considered her dad's reaction. He'd be hurt. Disappointed.

"What should I do, Mom?"

But she already knew. There was no longer any way for her to put her dad's feelings over hers. Not this time. It was too huge—her entire future banked on whether she was honest with him or not. And, of course, whether Zach still wanted her.

She slowly got to her feet. Reaching out, she touched the cold, wet stone one last time, reluctant to break the connection.

"I'll be back, Mom."

CHAPTER TWENTY

THE BLAST OF THE CIVIC'S heater couldn't begin to warm Lindsey. Not only was she dripping wet clear through, but chills ran down her spine at the thought of the upcoming conversation with her dad.

She pulled up at the curb in front of his house all too soon. The house was mostly dark, but it appeared Claudia's light was still on in her bedroom. Lindsey's dad may have gone to bed.

Too bad. She was going to get this out in the open tonight.

Lindsey let herself in the front door, trying to ignore the dread deep in her gut. Setting her coat on the bottom step, she quickly made her way up the stairs.

Claudia's door was partially open, and she was sitting up in bed, reading.

"Hi," Lindsey said quietly.

"Thought I heard someone come in. Oh, honey, you're soaked!"

Lindsey nodded absently. "Went to the cemetery. I need to talk to Dad."

"I think he's asleep." Claudia stuck a bookmark in her place in the book and set it on the nightstand. "You okay?"

Lindsey met her gaze. "I will be. I'm going to wake him up."

She ducked out before Claudia could ask more questions.

LINDSEY PACED BACK AND FORTH across the worn living room carpet, waiting for her dad and Claudia to join her. Finally, they made their way down the stairs, with Claudia holding on to his arm.

"What's going on, Lindsey?" Her dad was still sleepy. "Why are you drenched?"

"I've been…outside," she said. "Have a seat."

Lindsey sat in the armchair facing the couch, where the couple sat together.

Abruptly, she sprung from the chair, unable to sit still. As she walked toward the fireplace they rarely used, she said,

"I'm not sure where to start or how to say this...."

"What is it, dear?" Claudia's worry was evident.

Lindsey took a fortifying breath. "It's Zach. I'm in love with him."

Her dad leaned forward, resting his arms on his thighs, bowing his head. He seemed to deflate.

Claudia took hold of his forearm, as if she expected him to explode. He didn't, though. He didn't say a thing for the longest time, and Lindsey just stood there, clenching her hands, her heart pounding.

So much rode on his reaction. He could kick her out of his life for good. The thought made her feel like withering into a ball on the floor. But she wouldn't. She'd gone into this fully aware that the consequences could be ugly. It was a chance she'd had to take.

"Zach Rundle." He didn't look at her. Didn't phrase it as a question. Just a statement.

She nodded, pointlessly, since his head was still bowed and he couldn't see her.

"You knew about this, Claudia, didn't you?"

Her grip tightened on his arm as she shook her head. "I told you it wouldn't surprise me, though."

Finally, he met Lindsey's eyes. "What am I supposed to do?"

"What?"

"What do you expect from me, Lindsey? Should I jump up and hug you?" His voice remained calm, but there was a hint of anger behind the words.

"Not unless you feel like hugging me." Which, clearly, he didn't. "Dad, I know you don't like their family. Believe me, I fought my feelings for a long time because I didn't want to upset you."

"And what? In the end, you decided 'to hell with him, so what if he can't take it?'"

"Wendell." Claudia tried to reel him in before he got carried away. From the look on her dad's face, she had her work cut out.

"I'll tell you exactly what I decided, Dad. Because it was a long time coming, and it wasn't an easy decision. There are things you should know."

"Like what, that you've been sneaking behind our backs to see him? That you crept over there in the dead of night? Is that why you were so willing to stay with me while Claudia was gone?"

"No! I've cared for Zach for years. Since before Mom died. When Claudia left town, I was trying to tell myself he's the awful person you think he is. Didn't work. Because he's not."

"You said there are things we should know," Claudia said calmly.

Lindsey sucked in a full breath of air. She sat on the arm of the chair. "I don't think you'll like them."

"Can it get any worse?" Her dad stood and walked to the fireplace.

"I went to Mom's grave tonight."

Her dad turned.

"Oh, Lindsey," Claudia said.

The other woman's sympathy made Lindsey falter. The urge to bury her face in her arms and let the threatening tears fall was powerful. But she had to get this all out.

"I'd forgotten so much. Especially the night she died." Her throat threatened to swell shut and cut off her air. "All these years I'd refused to remember. It hurt so bad to think about it, I just…didn't."

Claudia nodded. Lindsey didn't dare look at her dad.

"The thing is…I felt guilty for Mom's accident."

"No," Claudia said quietly.

"I know. He was drunk. But still…I'm the one who begged her to go to a movie. And I was driving."

"It wasn't your fault." Her dad's voice was gruff, barely audible. She glanced at him and saw tears in his eyes.

She hugged her arms across her chest. "I felt like I needed to make up for the accident. Fix everything here. For you, Dad."

He stared at her without a word.

"Oh, honey," Claudia said.

"I didn't understand any of this until recently. I was so incapable of admitting my feelings for Zach. Didn't want to disappoint you. Didn't want to hurt you more. I'd already caused enough pain."

"Hellfire." Her dad uttered the oath under his breath. He rubbed both hands over his face wearily. "Honey. I wish I'd known."

Hope sparked inside her.

"I wish I'd known, too, Dad, trust me."

"None of it was your fault. You were my little girl when it happened. I never blamed you." He moved toward her. "Come here."

She stepped into his arms, tears blinding her. They held on to each other, and Lindsey heard sniffles from Claudia. If he was hugging her, he wouldn't send her away, would he?

When her dad finally pulled back, she wiped her eyes.

"I don't want to hear any more about the accident being remotely your fault. You hear me?"

She nodded tentatively. "I'm working on it. Going to the cemetery helped."

"I'm glad you went." He made his way to Claudia's side and lowered himself back to the couch. "About…Zach." She could see him swallow. "It's hard for me."

"I wish you'd get to know him, Dad." She sat back in the chair.

"It's a gut reaction. I hear that name, that last name, and it ties my insides into a knot."

Sadness balled in her chest and fresh tears came to her eyes. Because she understood.

"I'll admit I don't know the first thing about him. He was a pain in the butt growing up, if I remember right."

Lindsey's lips edged up. "He's matured. Going to adopt his nephew."

Her dad watched her closely. "His brother too drunk to be a father?" His words dripped with disdain.

"Basically."

"I'm glad Zach's going to take care of him," Claudia said. "Poor kid."

"He's going to be a great dad. There's no question in my mind," Lindsey said.

"And you're going to mother this child? Josh's child?" Her dad's voice was quiet, even, without blatant censure.

She hadn't even thought that far yet, she'd been so caught up in Zach and then confronting her dad. "Y-yes. I guess I am. If Zach will have me. We…aren't actually together right now. I don't know what he'll say when I talk to him."

Both older people studied her in silence. Lindsey fought the urge to pop up off the chair and pace.

"I can see it in your face when you talk about him, you love him," her dad said.

"If I'd had my say in the man who would steal your heart, it wouldn't have been a Rundle. But I'd be a clod not to give you my blessing."

Then she did burst off the chair and rushed across the living room to throw her arms around him. Again, tears fell. Hers and Claudia's.

"Thank you, Dad."

He cleared his throat as she straightened. "I can't promise to be his biggest fan. But I'll give him a chance."

"That's all I ask for." She hugged him one more time.

"Just let me take it slow. Can you do that?"

She wiped her eyes and nodded. "I love you, Dad."

"Love you, too. Now go find out if that man is smart enough to take you back."

She bent down to hug Claudia and ran to the door. To find out if she had a future with Zach.

LINDSEY DIDN'T BOTHER GOING to her car. She traipsed across the front yard, relieved the Rundles' house was still lit. She knew

Zach would be up at this hour, but she hated to wake Mrs. Rundle or Owen.

She tapped lightly on the heavy wood door. She couldn't guess how Zach would react to seeing her here. It could go either way, but even if he tried to send her away again, she had every intention of making him hear her out. Tonight.

She knocked again, louder. Footsteps approached on the other side, but they didn't sound like Zach at all. Too light. The door eased open and a woman she'd never seen before smiled politely.

"Hi. I was looking for Zach."

The woman's smile warmed. "I'm afraid he's not here."

"Do you know what time he'll be home?" She hadn't realized his truck wasn't in the driveway.

"He took Owen to Wichita."

Lindsey's heart sank.

Mrs. Rundle shuffled up behind the woman, wearing an old, threadbare robe. "Lindsey? Is that you?"

"I wanted to talk to Zach, but I hear he's gone."

The older woman smiled kindly as she

came to a stop right next to the other woman, whoever she was. "Whatcha need, hon?"

Lindsey glanced at the woman she didn't know.

"This is Annie. She's my new babysitter."

"Caregiver," Annie corrected. "Nice to meet you."

"You, too." Lindsey forced a smile, even though she just wanted to get out of there now that she knew Zach wasn't home.

"What do you need to talk to Zachary about?" Mrs. Rundle asked again.

"It's…personal."

Zach's grandma looked her over carefully, knowingly. Her attitude toward Lindsey had changed over the past few weeks, and they'd stumbled onto a mutual tolerance of each other. Lindsey had a hard time hating a woman who had such a terrible future awaiting her. And really, she was a decent woman inside; the crusty facade just threw a lot of people off.

Still, Lindsey wasn't comfortable enough to pour her heart out to her.

"He's at his apartment in Wichita. Went back for the commission meeting tonight. You could drive down there yourself—1912, Ashland Drive. Apartment three."

"It's getting late. It can wait," she lied. "Thank you. Sorry to bother you."

"Don't you worry about it. Some things are pressing." She actually winked at Lindsey, who pretended she didn't see it and turned to leave.

Now what?

She shivered. She was still soaked to the bone. A hot shower sounded like the best place to start. She'd have to wait till tomorrow to track Zach down and see if he really loved her or had already given up.

CHAPTER TWENTY-ONE

LINDSEY WATCHED HER digital clock turn to 3:30 a.m. just as she'd watched it turn to three and two and so on. She sat up and whipped the covers aside. If she lay here another minute, she would go certifiably crazy.

She wandered into the spare bedroom Brooke used as an office. Turning on the desktop computer, she sat at the desk.

The address Mrs. Rundle had rattled off earlier was still fresh in Lindsey's mind. She typed in the address of a mapping Web site and then entered the address. Voilà. Directions to Zach's doorstep.

She stared at the screen for a good five minutes, considering her options. Sleep wasn't going to come anytime soon. The longer she sat around in the dark, the more she would think about her mom, her dad. Zach. Thinking was getting her nowhere.

If she left now, she'd get there by about six-thirty, in time to catch him before he went to work. And then some.

She checked her planner for morning appointments. She had a meeting with her supervisor that she could postpone. Her in-home meetings weren't until the evening. She could make it back to Lone Oak in time for them.

Snapping into action, she clicked Print, waited for the map to slide out of the printer and returned to her bedroom to get dressed. She threw on dry jeans, a tank and her favorite fuzzy hooded sweater. More comfort clothes.

Before she left, she threw a toothbrush in her purse and scribbled a note to Brooke, who'd probably be up in the next couple hours, anyway.

NEARLY THREE HOURS LATER she was in Wichita and still alert, thanks to a forty-four ounce vat of caffeine. That, and the anticipation of seeing Zach.

Lindsey drove into an all-night gas

station that was lit brighter than a baseball stadium during a night game. She studied the map until she knew the rest of the route and got back on the road, which was mostly deserted.

The sky was just starting to lighten, and either the rain from last night had stopped or she'd driven out of it. The sidewalks and streets were dry, but the air was chilly, especially after the cocoon of warmth in the car.

Zach's apartment was one of four units in a well-maintained brick building. Bland but functional. She found number three on the ground floor. Lindsey's heart beat erratically as she walked toward the door.

She knocked at number three, her heart in her throat. She shivered and waited for ages, then knocked again. Finally, on the third knock, the door opened.

Zach scowled out at her through drowsy eyes, his hair a mess. He wore boxers and nothing else, and the room behind him was dark. Lindsey held back the urge to run into his arms.

"Wha—? Lindsey? What the hell?"

Her fingers itched to touch his bare

chest, to run her hands over his pecs then wind her arms around him. But she couldn't tell anything about his thoughts. All she knew was she'd woken him up and he was surprised to see her.

"Can I come in?"

Without a word, he opened the door wider and stood back. "What time is it?"

"Six-thirtyish. Sorry I woke you."

Zach walked past her to a couch he'd apparently used as a bed, judging by the blankets and pillow on it. He sat next to the pillow and reached over to turn on the lamp on the end table.

The couch was the only piece of furniture to sit on in the room. "Mind if I—?" It was awkward to be so formal with him.

Zach patted the cushion next to him. "What's going on? Why are you here?"

"Your grandma said you brought Owen to Wichita."

"He's in my bedroom."

"You gave him your bed? That's so sweet."

He leveled a sleepy look at her. "Why are you here, Linds?"

Where to start? She'd had three hours

of solitude—and thrashing music—to figure out what to say, but she was far from prepared.

"I went to the cemetery last night." She couldn't afford to lose it right now. "Sat at my mom's grave for a long time. Thought about a lot of things."

"That must've been difficult."

Lindsey nodded. "I don't want to feel guilty anymore." She could feel the heat of his bare leg through her jeans.

"I...told my dad I care about you." Once the words were out she looked at him.

His expression suddenly became alert. "Bet that went over well," he said carefully.

"Actually, a whole lot better than I'd expected. I knew telling him could mean being forced out of his life. I was prepared for that, and I'd still be here even if that had happened. But...he gave me his blessing. Said he would try to get to know you." She pulled her sleeves down over her hands and pulled one leg up under her. "I owe you an apology."

His eyes narrowed.

"I've put my dad's feelings above yours forever. Didn't even consider how I made you feel." She wove her fingers with his and rested both of their hands on Zach's bare thigh. "I'm so sorry."

"It's okay," he said quietly.

"It's not. At all. I can't change the past but I'd like…" She met his gaze. "I'd like to make up for it."

His lips curved upward as he seemed to grasp why she was there. "How you going to do that?"

"However you'll let me."

His eyes got a hungry look to them.

"I love you, Zach. That's what I told my dad."

"I don't know what to say."

"You could start by telling me you love me, too."

"I do." He smiled, then frowned just as quickly. "You're sure things are okay with your dad? I don't want to come between you."

"I tried to play it his way, Zach. I was miserable. So…whether you want to see how things go with me or not, my dad knows how I feel."

"I want to see how things go." His voice was so low and sexy she wasn't sure she heard him right. "Screw that," he said, with more animation. "I want you. The good and the bad. We'll make it go."

Emotions threatened to overwhelm her and she found it difficult to sit still. "I thought about it the whole way here, and I'm sure I can get a similar job in Wichita."

Zach pulled her into a hug. Finally. Lindsey still longed to be closer so she crawled to straddle his lap. At last, she touched his chest and leaned in to kiss him.

He came up for air before she was ready. "There's one problem with your plan," he said huskily.

Her heart skipped a beat.

"Owen and I are moving to Lone Oak."

She stared at him. "You are?"

"I need to be near Gram, and Lone Oak's the closest thing Owen has to a home."

Lindsey let that sink in for a few seconds. Maybe minutes.

"What about your job? The company you want to buy?"

"We had our meeting with the commission last night. We won. The development is on."

"Congratulations. I know how much that means to you."

"I told Chuck I'm leaving."

She tilted her head in surprise.

"I've been saving my money for years to buy Moxley. Instead, I'm going to use it to start my own company in Lone Oak. I can do this. I'm good at what I do. Just changing where I do it."

"You'll have to start from scratch, though, Zach."

"It'll be *my* company." He brushed her hair back behind her shoulder. "I'll build it up. I helped Chuck build Moxley." He was excited about the prospect. His body language said so.

"You'll do it. I have no doubt," she said. "So tell me. What will Gram say about all this. About me?"

"She gives you a thumbs-up. You'll just have to get used to her kind of affection."

Lindsey laughed. "Something along the lines of anti-affection?"

"She's quite a woman. I hope you can get to know her better."

"I'd like that."

She frowned, not wanting to bring up her last doubt. But she had to. "What about Josh?"

"He's gone, Linds. He called on his way to Wyoming. Found a job on a ranch out there and is going to start over."

"Owen's his son. What if he wants to see him?"

"He agreed to sign away his rights. I told him he can visit but he's my son now. Our son…that is, if you'd like…. Don't worry about that yet. We'll work through it when we have to."

She could do that. With Zach at her side, she felt like she could do just about anything. "I'd love to adopt Owen with you."

Zach took her hand in his. "That'll make Owen the happiest kid in the world. One other thing I've been thinking about…"

"More?"

"Billy. Find a family for him yet?"

"Zach." Tears came to her eyes. "You think we should adopt him too?"

"It's crossed my mind. I wasn't sure I could handle two boys by myself, but with you…. Let's talk about it soon."

She hugged him tightly again, unable to speak for the emotion in her throat. Her tears dripped onto his bare shoulder. Twenty-four hours ago, she would've never believed she could be this happy.

"You're crying again?" Zach chuckled. "What's it going to take to make you stop?" He brushed his lips over her temple.

She laughed and sobbed at the same time. "You'll get used to it, I promise."

"Think long and hard before you go kissing me and chattering about the future, Linds. I come with some extras—a little boy and an old woman. You think you can handle all of us?"

"Let's see." She wiped her eyes, sat up and pretended to ponder. "The boy's a piece of cake, the woman's a teddy bear in disguise. And the man?" She stared intently into his eyes. "As soon as the little boy isn't in the next room, I'll show you exactly how well I can handle the man."

"As long as you keep on showing me for the rest of our lives."

Instead of answering him, Lindsey leaned in and kissed him for all she was worth.

* * * * *

Happily ever after is just the beginning...

Turn the page for a sneak preview of
A HEARTBEAT AWAY
by
Eleanor Jones

Harlequin Everlasting—Every great love
has a story to tell.™
A brand-new series
from Harlequin Books

Special? A prickle ran down my neck and my heart started to beat in my ears. Was today really special?

"Tuck in," he ordered.

I turned my attention to the feast that he had spread out on the ground. Thick, home-cooked ham sandwiches, sausage rolls fresh from the oven and a huge variety of mouthwatering scones and pastries. Hunger pangs took over, and I closed my eyes and bit into soft home-made bread.

When we were finally finished, I lay back against the bluebells with a groan, clutching my stomach.

Daniel laughed. "Your eyes are bigger than your stomach," he told me.

I leaned across to deliver a punch to his arm, but he rolled away, and when my fist met fresh air I collapsed in a fit of giggles before relaxing on my back and staring up into the flawless blue sky. We lay like that for quite a while, Daniel and I, side by side in companionable silence, until he stretched out his hand in an arc that encompassed the whole area.

"Don't you think that this is the most beautiful place in the entire world?"

His voice held a passion that echoed my own feelings, and I rose onto my elbow and picked a buttercup to hide the emotion that clogged my throat.

"Roll over onto your back," I urged, prodding him with my forefinger. He obliged with a broad grin, and I reached across to place the yellow flower beneath his chin.

"Now, let us see if you like butter."

When a yellow light shone on the tanned skin below his jaw, I laughed.

"There...you do."

For an instant our eyes met, and I had the strangest sense that I was drowning in those honey-brown depths. The scent of bluebells engulfed me. A roaring filled my ears, and then, unexpectedly, in one smooth movement Daniel rolled me onto my back and plucked a buttercup of his own.

"And do *you* like butter, Lucy McTavish?" he asked. When he placed the flower against my skin, time stood still.

His long lean body was suspended over mine, pinning me against the grass. Daniel…dear, comfortable, familiar Daniel was suddenly bringing out in me the strangest sensations.

"Do you, Lucy McTavish?" he asked again, his voice low and vibrant.

My eyes flickered toward his, the whisper of a sigh escaped my lips and although a strange lethargy had crept into my limbs, I somehow felt as if all my nerve endings were on fire. He felt it, too—I could see it in his warm brown eyes. And when he lowered his face to mine, it seemed to me the most natural thing in the world.

None of the kisses I had ever experienced could have even begun to prepare me for the feel of Daniel's lips on mine. My entire body floated on a tide of ecstasy that shut out everything but his soft, warm mouth, and I knew that this was what I had been waiting for the whole of my life.

"Oh, Lucy." He pulled away to look into my eyes. "Why haven't we done this before?"

Holding his gaze, I gently touched his cheek, then I curled my fingers through the short thick hair at the base of his skull, overwhelmed by the longing to drown again in the sensations that flooded our bodies. And when his long tanned fingers crept across my tingling skin, I knew I could deny him nothing.

* * * * *

Be sure to look for
A HEARTBEAT AWAY,
available February 27, 2007.

And look, too, for
THE DEPTH OF LOVE
by Margot Early,
the story of a couple who must learn
that love comes in many guises—
and in the end
it's the only thing that counts.

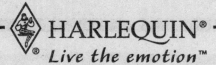

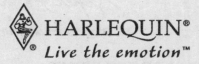

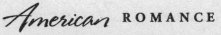
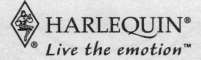

 Harlequin® Historical
Historical Romantic Adventure!

*Imagine a time of chivalrous
knights and unconventional ladies,
roguish rakes and impetuous
heiresses, rugged cowboys
and spirited frontierswomen——
these rich and vivid tales will
capture your imagination!*

*Harlequin Historical . . .
they're too good to miss!*

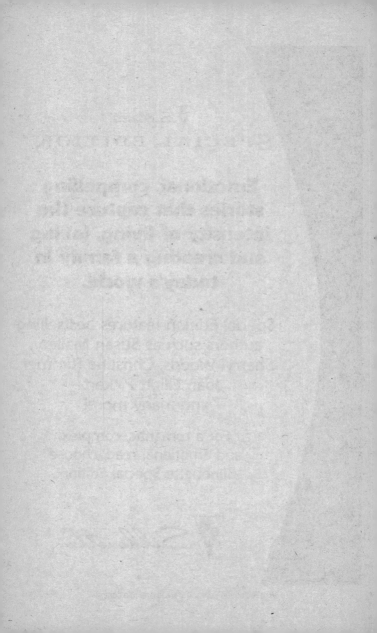